MONSTER HIGH™

SCHOOL SPIRITS #1

A FRIGHT TO REMEMBER

ADRIANNA CUEVAS

AMULET BOOKS · NEW YORK

Cataloging-in-Publication Data has been applied for and may be obtained from the Library of Congress.

ISBN 978-1-4197-6986-3

MONSTER HIGH™ and associated trademarks and trade dress are owned by, and used under license from, Mattel. © 2023 Mattel.

Text by Adrianna Cuevas
Book design by Brann Garvey

Printed and bound in U.S.A.

10 9 8 7 6 5 4 3 2 1

Amulet Books are available at special discounts when purchased in quantity for premiums and promotions as well as fundraising or educational use. Special editions can also be created to specification. For details, contact specialsales@abramsbooks.com or the address below.

Amulet Books® is a registered trademark of Harry N. Abrams, Inc.

ABRAMS The Art of Books
195 Broadway, New York, NY 10007
abramsbooks.com

For all the kids figuring out who they are
and looking for a place to belong

PROLOGUE

✧ 💀 ✧

In a corner of the city, far away from prying eyes and wandering strangers, sat a small, two-story building. Should anyone happen to walk past the building, they would barely register the shape of a house, as creeping vines covered the brick, and overgrown bushes blocked the windows. The building's most notable feature was a small statue of a lion perched outside the front gate. But even that was covered with twisting vines.

Surely no one lives here, passersby would tell themselves. *Surely, it's abandoned.*

But they'd be wrong.

Someone did live there—a woman who spent her days hunched over notebooks and laboratory equipment, plotting and scheming. She passed her nights pacing the halls of the worn-down house until the socks on her feet were threadbare and full of holes.

She had a singular mission. And she was running out of time.

The woman's hands fidgeted over a vial, a bright green liquid shining inside. Before she could pour her concoction into a beaker, the woman doubled over, wrapping her arm around her stomach. Her chest heaved as a coughing fit racked her body.

"I can't fail again," she mumbled, wiping her mouth with the back of her hand.

Pouring the green solution into a beaker filled with clear liquid, she grabbed a notebook on her table, searching for an empty page. She flipped past equations and diagrams. She scanned scribblings she hoped no one would ever read.

Her muscles grew heavy on her bones as she slumped onto her stool. Her breath caught in her throat as the bright green liquid slowly turned black as it mixed in the beaker. Letting her hand slide across the table, she knocked the now-useless concoction to the floor, the glass shattering in a splatter of glistening pieces.

"No, not again," the woman said, her voice barely a whisper.

She gave in to the blackness overwhelming her

senses and laid her head on the table, closing her eyes one final time.

Across the city, through the woods, and over the rolling hills sat another building that went largely unnoticed by the general public. But it wasn't climbing vines or overgrown plants that kept it hidden—it was a power that emanated from deep within the building. The only ones who could see the structure, the only ones who could access it, were ones who belonged.

Monsters.

The students at Monster High were used to their school having a life of its own. Staircases wandered to nowhere, rooms disappeared and reappeared, and mirrors provided access to whole other worlds.

But as the students went to their classes, had pickup games on the casketball court, and dared each other to try the latest culinary creation in the creepateria, there was one thing they didn't know, one thing only the most observant monster could realize.

As the woman across town took her last breath, something deep inside Monster High woke up.

CHAPTER 1

Talent shows at human schools typically involved songs that were best sung in the shower, dubious magic tricks with rebellious rabbits, and stand-up comedians telling groan-worthy dad jokes.

But Monster High was no human school.

When Headmistress Bloodgood announced the annual talent show last week, the halls buzzed with electricity. All the students were busy practicing their routines, selecting their performances, and evaluating one another's skills. The school was alive with excitement. Each monster was eager to exhibit their talent with pride, far from curious human eyes.

In a corner of the Monster High kitchen, Deuce Gorgon was perfecting the decorations of his three-tiered cake. He created dark green buttercream and piped it on as snakes slithering up the sides of the cake.

"That doesn't look like usss," Pride, one of the snakes on Deuce's head, said as it peeked out from underneath his gray ski cap.

"We have better ssscales," Envy hissed, sliding out from behind Deuce's ear.

Deuce sighed and mumbled under his breath, "You know, having the seven deadly snakes on your head means seven critics of everything you do."

Before he could defend his work, the snakes knocked Deuce's glasses off and yellow lasers shot out from his eyes. His creation immediately turned from soft cake and fluffy icing to hard stone.

"Aw, c'mon dudes! I would've let you have a piece!" Deuce groaned, tossing his piping bag on the table.

As he headed over to the kitchen's garbage goblin, which stomped its feet on the floor in excitement to gobble up Deuce's stone cake, he slipped on a puddle of water that had seeped underneath the door.

"Lagoona! Your talent is leaking!" Deuce called through the door and down the hall.

Popping her head out from one of Monster High's many practice rooms that had appeared once the talent show was announced, Lagoona Blue covered her mouth with a laugh. "Ay, sorry, Deuce!"

Lagoona was busy creating sculptures of her latest crush. She shot water out of her webbed hands in intricate patterns that held themselves in place, making liquid figures that looked like glass. Just as she finished perfecting the swoop of the fins that protruded from the top of Gil Weber's head, she stepped back and examined her art. Lagoona had decided to make a sculpture of the fresh-water monster after she'd heard him practice his singing for the talent show.

"Oh, he's so perfect, I could just kidnap him and keep him forever!" Lagoona had exclaimed while Gil sang, her pupils narrowing into thin slits as her sharp teeth grew.

Only, once she finished her water sculpture, Lagoona wasn't sure if the piece really did Gil justice.

"Ay, Dios mío, it has to be absolutely perfect!" Lagoona yelped. "Gil is just so cute, I could eat him up!"

Lagoona tiptoed down the hallway and peeked in on Heath practicing for the talent show. He was giving a speech about the importance of recycling at Monster High. But he kept getting too passionate about his topic, sending flames shooting from his hair and catching the curtains on fire (a downside to being the son of Hades). The window in his practice room immediately opened on its own, letting the rain from the storm outside blow across the curtains and douse the fire.

Just as the last of the flames vanished from the singed curtains, Cleo DeNile, Monster High's most fashionable mummy, walked by scrolling through EekTok on her iCoffin.

"Oh, juggling is trending. I bet I could do that," she said, biting her lip. "Maybe I could use the jars with my organs. That would impress everyone."

Her iCoffin beeped, and Cleo sighed. "Oh, for the love of Ra. It's not trending anymore. Let's see. Now sword-swallowing is number one. I wonder how quickly I can learn that."

The daughter of the Mummy shuffled away, her golden shoes clacking on the hallway tiles, determined to find the talent that would bring her the most fame.

As the students of Monster High planned, practiced, and perfected, there was one student who was certain they'd found an amazing routine—one that would knock the bolts, fins, and wings off everyone in attendance.

Frankie Stein.

As music from Frankie's keytar floated down the hallway, the light fixtures on the walls bounced to the rhythm. Frankie's fingers slid over the neck of the keytar, a growl emanating from its strings. Their fingers tickled over the keys, a melody filling the dorm room Frankie shared with Clawdeen Wolf and Draculaura.

With one final swing of their arm, Frankie smashed their fingers down on the keys, sparks shooting from each nail and bouncing up the neck of the keytar, electrifying its strings.

When the song finished, Frankie looked expectantly at their iCoffin. "Well, what do you think?" they asked.

No words came from the iCoffin. Only claps, cheers, and shouts from Frankie's parents, the Doctors Mary and Victor Stein.

A wide smile broke out on Frankie's face as they laid their keytar aside on their bed.

"Woo-hoo!" Frankie's dad shouted. "That was spooktacular!"

"You'd win Song of the Year at the Screamys if it was up to me," Frankie's mom added.

Frankie laughed. "Zaps! You really think so?"

"Oh, we know so," Frankie's parents blurted out at the same time, wide smiles on their faces.

Frankie's parents, both scientists, had created Frankie just weeks ago and enrolled them immediately at Monster High. Because, of course, only the best monster school would do for their monster child. It had taken Frankie a little while to get used to not only their new school but also just being in existence!

Clawdeen and Draculaura helped a lot when Frankie got confused about the ins and outs of Monster High (like explaining that Headmistress Bloodgood wasn't *literally* talking about the ocean when she said Frankie looked like "a fish out of water," or that nothing bad was going to happen to Lagoona when she said Gil was "to die for").

Frankie ran their fingers through the blue streak in their hair and shrugged. "Wasn't too sure what talent I should do. All these different parts in my brain were trying to convince me they'd be the best pick. Do you think it would be okay to train piranhas on stage? That's what my marine biologist brain part says."

Frankie's mom shook her head. "I don't think Headmistress Bloodgood would appreciate that."

Frankie's parents had selected different sections of brain from the best thinkers and creators in the world, both human and monster, to make Frankie. Chemists, mathematicians, musicians, artists, biologists—Frankie's brain was overflowing with ideas and information. It felt amazing to have a brain buzzing with parts from the world's smartest minds. Even if that made things kind of noisy sometimes.

Frankie's parents laughed, their faces filling up the screen of the iCoffin. "Oh, my valiant little volt, you'll be fantastic no matter what talent you pick," Frankie's dad said.

"Now go break a leg!" Frankie's mom cheered.

Frankie raised an eyebrow. "Don't think breaking my legs is a talent anyone wants to see. And if I did, I guess I could repair them and show off the bionic legs I created."

Frankie's parents smiled and waved at them. "We love you, Frankie!"

"Love you, Mom and Dad!" Frankie said, disconnecting the call.

They picked up their keytar again and practiced the opening measures of the song they'd chosen for the talent show, the music floating out the open door of the dorm room and down the hall.

What Frankie didn't see while they were focused on their parents was the face of Toralei Stripe smirking as she recorded Frankie playing their keytar. Toralei had been walking down the hallway when she heard the music coming from Frankie's room. She stopped and listened as Frankie created different rhythms with each hand on the keytar. But then Frankie finished their song and their parents cheered, clapping and praising Frankie. Heat rose to Toralei's cheeks as she seethed and gripped her iCoffin in her hand. She rolled her eyes. Toralei's parents never talked to her like that. It was only ever about how their werecat family was superior to humans, and even to a lot of other monsters.

"I wonder what everyone really thinks of your routine. We'll see who's so happy after this," she huffed, pressing share on her phone with more force than necessary.

Now all Toralei had to do was wait.

CHAPTER 2

✿💀✿

Watzie, the key signature we're looking for is A flat major. That's exactly what this new song needs," Frankie told their pet as he hopped on the stone pattern that made up the dorm room floor.

Watzie, a gray-and-black dog with electric blue wings sprouting from his back, barked in agreement as a small circular stone by the corner of Frankie's bed lifted slightly. Sniffing the now-moving floor with his nose, Watzie crooked his neck in curiosity.

"That occipital lobe from a banshee composer sure is useful," Frankie said, pointing to the back of their head.

Another stone from the floor shook, and Watzie ran over to investigate. He sniffed and barked, but Frankie was completely engrossed in the keytar sitting on their lap and the sheet music spread across their green bedspread.

Watzie's electric wings flashed a bright blue as three more stones shook and lifted from the floor. Watzie barked and ran over to Frankie, licking their black combat boot and sending sparks across the leather.

"What is it, buddy?" Frankie asked, setting their keytar aside on the bed.

Watzie scampered over to the uneven section of floor and hopped up on the stones that had risen.

Looking at Watzie, Frankie's neck immediately straightened, and their eyes opened wide. "A level sub-floor will ensure the structural integrity of a building," they blurted out. "Any unevenness will exponentially increase with height."

Watzie barked and nodded in agreement as Frankie let out a whooshing breath. "Wow. That bit of chupacabra architect is loud today."

Different parts of Frankie's brain were known to nudge Frankie pretty hard—and sometimes shout—when stimulated by something familiar. Just the right painting shown by Mrs. O'Shriek in monster arts class could make Frankie blurt out that the difference between a tint, a tone, and a shade was whether white, gray, or black had been added to the color—all thanks to a poltergeist portrait artist brain part. Or Frankie might instantly inform everyone in the creepateria that broccoli evolved from wild cabbage after seeing a fish and vegetable-filled stinkwich, care of a botanist brain part.

Frankie couldn't always control when their different brain parts decided to speak up. Their zombie mathematician brain part would shoot Frankie's hand up to answer a question in clawculus class. Their award-winning human chemist brain part would take over experiments in boo-ology. Sometimes, Frankie couldn't help but wonder when they'd get a chance to use their own voice.

"BOO!"

Frankie looked up and spotted Spectra Vondergeist poking halfway out of the ceiling, her arms waving and her face contorted in a snarl.

"Oh, hi, Spectra," Frankie said, poking a finger at the stone that had risen from the floor and was now trembling slightly.

Spectra lowered her arms. "You weren't scared?" she asked, defeated. She blew a strand of white hair off her forehead.

Frankie shrugged. "Not really. That's the tenth time today that you've tried to scare me. It's expected."

"Ugh!" Spectra groaned, her dark purple dress floating in the air. "How am I supposed to show off my scaring skills at the talent show now?"

Spectra disappeared into the ceiling with a faint moan. Frankie chuckled.

Before they could investigate the cause of the uneven floor, their roommates Draculaura and Clawdeen came into the room.

"Um, Frankie, have you been on EekTok today?" Draculaura asked, sitting next to Frankie on their bed. She flipped her pink-and-black hair over her shoulder, small fangs protruding from her mouth as she smiled uncertainly at her roommate.

Frankie shook their head, their fingers toying with the strings of their keytar, which they'd laid next to them on the bed. "Not really. Did I miss something? Did Cleo post another makeup tutorial? She really has the best looks, don't you think? Oh! Did Deuce's snake Sloth post another video of him slithering up Deuce's nose while he was sleeping?"

Clawdeen sniffed the air, activating her super werewolf sense of smell. "No, Deuce is still cooking right now. Oh, maybe he'd make us some vanilla cupsnakes with screamberry icing!"

Draculaura put her hand on Frankie's shoulder. "No, it's not cupsnakes, makeup tutorials, or anything like that. It's this."

Holding out her iCoffin to Frankie, Draculaura played a video from EekTok.

"That's me!" Frankie exclaimed, pointing to the video of their keytar routine.

"We know," Clawdeen said, sitting down on the floor in front of Frankie. Her pale pink–and–bright fuchsia hair cascaded over her shoulders. She wrapped one curl around her finger. "And we think you're absolutely clawsome. But Toralei didn't exactly post the nicest caption about your playing."

Frankie took Draculaura's iCoffin and watched Toralei's video again. It already had a thousand views. Then they read the caption Toralei wrote.

Keytar playing is so four decades ago. So cringe.

Purrsephone, Toralei's underling, commented directly underneath. *I would be so embarrassed if that was my talent.*

Meowlody, another one of Toralei's crew, added, *Better to not perform in the show at all if this is what you're gonna do. Yikes.*

Frankie took a deep breath and handed Draculaura's iCoffin back to her. The butterflies in their stomach started flying around in swirls, making Frankie pull on a loose thread dangling from their plaid skirt. The mechanical butterflies usually worked to help distribute electricity throughout Frankie's body, but sometimes they overreacted when Frankie got nervous. "They don't like my playing?"

Clawdeen jumped to her feet and put her hands on her hips, pushing her glasses up the bridge of her nose with her finger. "Some monsters don't under-stand music. And some monsters should think twice before meeting me on the casketball court, in case I dunk them straight into another realm. Just saying."

Draculaura looked at Clawdeen and put her hands up, her bat-shaped earrings dangling back and forth. "Deep breath. Calm," she said, inhaling and exhaling in an exaggerated manner. "I know Toralei is prob-ably your least favorite monster in this entire school."

"Gah!" Clawdeen growled as she tried breathing slowly to calm down. "It's not my fault she's always making things up to get me kicked out of school. Or that her mom and my mom are enemies!"

Toralei's family hated humans and certainly didn't think they belonged at Monster High. Since Claw-deen's dad was human and her mom was a werewolf, Toralei had very strong opinions about whether she should be allowed at school. On top of that, Toralei's werecat family didn't get along with Clawdeen's were-wolf family. The tension started because Clawdeen's mom, Selena, used to be the Were-Ruler, but Torelei's mom took over while she was in another realm. It was like cats and dogs always hissing and barking at each other, just . . . monster-fied.

Draculaura nodded. "Drama. I get it. But let's focus on what Toralei did to Frankie right now, OK?"

Frankie frowned and twisted their hands in their lap. "Do you two like my playing?" they asked. Frankie cast a cautious glance at the keytar still laying on their bed. It was the first instrument they'd tried, and instantly it connected to their composer brain part. Frankie felt energized when they played, even more than the usual electric current running through their body.

"Oh, of course we do!" Draculaura said. "I mean, it may not be my favorite when I'm trying to study and you're shredding chords loud enough to wake the undead. But I love how happy your playing makes you."

Clawdeen nodded in agreement, sitting back down on the floor and crossing her legs. She played with the moonclaw necklace hanging down the front of her purple overalls. "No one can play like you can, Frankie. You're totally clawsome!"

"But Toralei's video had so many likes. Half the school agrees with her!" Frankie said. Everyone had been so welcoming when Frankie first came to school. Even with Frankie's misunderstandings and their tendency to blurt out random information, the students at Monster High treated them just like everyone else. But had Frankie been wrong? Had everyone just been hiding what they really thought?

"Do you think I should just find a different talent? Got lots of different brain parts to choose from, I guess," Frankie said with a sigh.

Draculaura patted Frankie's leg. "I know you can come up with something amazing. But only change your routine if you want to. It doesn't matter what Toralei says. What matters is you do a performance that makes you happy."

Frankie wanted to believe Draculaura. But Toralei's video and her mean comments kept playing on a loop in Frankie's brain (mostly because Frankie had a photographic memory). What Toralei said burrowed deep inside Frankie's heart, too. Frankie had done their best to adjust to everything at Monster High.

But none of their brain parts had prepared them for a situation like this.

After Draculaura and Clawdeen left the dorm room—Draculaura doing her best to keep Clawdeen from searching for Toralei so they could settle things then and there—Frankie still sat on their bed. The floor shook slightly under their feet as Watzie barked at yet another stone pushing its way up from the bumpy floor. But Frankie ignored it. All their brain parts were focused on something else.

"Gonna find a new talent," Frankie said, their fists clenched in determination. "And it's going to be the best talent ever!"

CHAPTER 3

🍀 💀 🍀

The following day, Frankie wandered the halls of Monster High, peeking in on other students' practices for the talent show. Deuce was still having trouble keeping his snakes from turning his sweet creations into stone. Lagoona couldn't settle on one singular crush to immortalize in sculpture. Cleo kept searching trending topics on EekTok for a talent idea. And Heath was still setting curtains on fire.

At least Spectra had only tried to scare them five times that day instead of the usual fifteen, but Frankie wished she hadn't popped out of the bathroom mirror while Frankie was washing their hands. Frankie splashed water all over the mirror, their shirt, and Spectra's hair. The water short-circuited Frankie's hand and a spark shot out at the lights, plunging the bathroom into darkness. That's probably why Spectra avoided Frankie for the rest of the day.

Now Frankie made their way to the library, a large box in their arms. It contained files full of information about their brain, who the various parts came, from and what they could do. Their parents had given the file to Frankie when they first started at Monster High so they could understand all their parts. Frankie loved looking through the box learning new information, and making improvements with bionic prosthetics.

Watzie scampered next to Frankie, trying to keep up but continually getting distracted by new doors appearing in each hallway. They all had signs on them that said OPEN ME! and THIS WAY!

Frankie didn't notice the doors over the large box they were carrying. Besides, they were on a mission.

"Well, hiya there, Frankie," Manny Taur said when Frankie entered the library. Manny towered over Frankie, his broad shoulders filling up the entire area behind the circulation desk. As Monster High's junior librarian, Manny loved being surrounded by books more than by other monsters. He was one of only a few students not participating in the talent show. While he was more than happy to help his classmates research information for their performances, he had absolutely no intention of getting up onstage in front of a whole group of monsters, thank you very much.

"Gotta lot of research to do," Frankie said, holding out an overflowing box to Manny. "Do you think there's a table to work at? I tried to work in my room, but the floor keeps shaking and sliding my papers everywhere."

A broad smile broke out on Manny's face. "Research is the best activity ever! I have the perfect place for you," Manny said, leading Frankie down an aisle of books. He squeezed his shoulders in to avoid knocking any books off the shelves, but several fell anyway. Frankie detached their hand from their wrist and shot it out on a long coil, catching each one quickly and placing them back on the shelf without Manny even noticing.

The only other monster in the library was Twyla Boogeyman, in her usual spot by the ghoulfather clock in the corner, twenty books stacked in front of her like a fort. Like Manny, she seemed more comfortable being around books than around other monsters.

"Best spot in the library right there. It's better than a hotdish smothered in cheese," Manny said, waving his hand at a long table under a tall window. Out the window was a view of the casketball court. Frankie smiled as they watched Clawdeen dribble down the court, jump in the air, and smash the ball through the small coffin perched on a large rock.

"Why would you heat up a dish and only put cheese on it?" Frankie asked.

"No, sorry, it's a casserole. Well, I mean . . . never mind," Manny said.

"Oh, okay. Well, thanks, Manny," Frankie said, spreading out the papers from their brain file. Watzie hopped up on a chair next to Frankie and sniffed an old, yellowed page.

At first, Frankie had no idea how to figure out a new talent. It wasn't until Watzie scampered out from underneath Frankie's bed, pushing a thick file with his nose, that Frankie realized they probably already knew the perfect talent. It was somewhere in one of their brain parts. They just had to find it.

Frankie read over several papers. Holding out one page, Frankie bit their lip. "This might be a good routine. Got a bit of parietal lobe from a French gargoyle seismologist."

An electric spark shot from Frankie's ears and their back straightened.

"*Oh, je voudrais tant que tu te souviennes, des jours heureux quand nous étions amis,*" Frankie said, their arms extended dramatically as if they were onstage.

Upon finishing, Frankie dropped their arms and looked at Watzie. His head was lowered on the table, a soft snore coming from his lips.

"OK, not that exciting," Frankie said with a slight groan. "Not sure why an earthquake scientist was so obsessed with poetry anyway. Maybe she could help me figure out why my room won't stop shaking instead."

Frankie rifled through the papers and picked up a new page. "Let's see what else is in here," they said, examining it closely and then turning the paper over to a blank side. Frankie grabbed a pencil from the library table.

"Hold still just a sec, Watzie," Frankie said, scrawling the pencil across the page. When they finished, they held their arm out and examined their drawing. "Do you think this looks like you, Watzie?"

Waking from his nap, Watzie looked at the drawing and perked his ears up, cocking his neck to the side with a grunt.

Frankie angled the page to the left, to the right, and even held it upside down. "You're right. It looks more like Kuma than you. Saving that bit of cerebellum from a poltergeist portrait artist for later, I guess."

Frankie pushed aside their drawing, reminding themself to give it to Monster High's only yōkai, since it looked like him doing what he did best—throwing huge boulders. The Japanese bear monster would probably hang it up next to his skull-put medals.

Watzie sniffed at the papers spread across the desk and nudged one over to Frankie with his nose. After reading it quickly, a spark shot from Frankie's neck. "This is a good one. Hang on."

Working quickly, Frankie pulled off the tie they were wearing over their white button-down shirt and used it to pull their black-, white-, and blue-streaked hair into a high ponytail. They slipped off their Monster High varsity jacket and secured it around their waist like a skirt over their ripped jeans. For the final touch, they loosened the laces on their black combat boots and rolled down the tops, revealing brightly colored striped socks. Hopping up on the library table, Frankie walked across its top, posing as if on the most famous Paris runway. They ended their performance by narrowing their eyes and pursing their lips into the perfect smize.

Striking a final pose, Frankie looked expectantly at Watzie. But he was occupied by a door that had suddenly appeared next to a bookshelf, a large sign on the front reading HERE! Watzie jumped down from the table, scampered over to the door, and scratched the wood with his paw. The door opened slightly, and Watzie peeked in. But whatever he saw inside made him squeak and run back to Frankie, pressing himself against their leg.

"Not that captivating, I guess," Frankie groaned, sitting down in a huff on top of the library table. "So, the siren fashion model's frontal lobe is a no."

Pulling their iCoffin from their jacket pocket, Frankie opened EekTok. They scrolled through several videos of students practicing their talent show performances. Cleo had made a video of her attempt at juggling all the jars that contained her organs, but it ended with Cleo groaning as the jar holding their liver smashed all over the floor.

Deuce was still having trouble with his snakes sabotaging his baking. This time, Gluttony devoured all twelve of Deuce's cupsnakes before he could decorate them.

Frankie smiled as a video of Draculaura singing a song from her favorite K-pop group, RTS, or Raising the Sirens, popped up. But then as Frankie scrolled, Toralei's EekTok video of their keytar practice popped up again. There were five times as many views as before, and a lot of the comments hadn't gotten better. Monsters that Frankie didn't even know were judging their playing.

Frankie tossed their phone on the table and put their head in their hands.

"Sorry to interrupt, but are you OK there, Frankie?" Manny asked as he slid a thick green book he had accidentally knocked onto the floor back on the shelf.

Frankie shrugged. "Just trying to find a routine for the talent show. Thought maybe something would come from researching my brain parts, but nothing here seems to fit. I was going to play keytar, but then Toralei . . ."

Frankie's voice trailed off.

Manny shoved his hands in the pockets of his khaki pants. His red sweater vest stretched across his broad chest. "I think you can say it. That video wasn't nice."

Frankie shrugged. "She was just giving me constructive criticism, right?"

Sitting down at the table next to Frankie, Manny sighed, his wide shoulders heaving. "I'm sorry if this sounds like I'm judging, but there's a difference between helping someone get better and being mean."

Frankie looked across the library, scanning all the shelves. "You wouldn't happen to have a chart that explains that, would you? Would be great to research it."

Manny looked at Frankie with a sympathetic smile. Before he could respond, Monster High's announcement system blared overhead. Skullette, the skull perched on the wall with a bright pink bow on its head, began to speak.

ATTENTION, STUDENTS! WOULD FRANKIE STEIN PLEASE PROCEED TO HEADMISTRESS BLOODGOOD'S OFFICE OR RISK BEING DEVOURED AND DECOMPOSED BY AN ACIDIC GOO MONSTER? OH . . . WAIT. SCRATCH THAT LAST PART. FRANKIE STEIN TO HEADMISTRESS BLOODGOOD'S OFFICE AS QUICKLY AS POSSIBLE.

CHAPTER 4

✢ 💀 ✢

Frankie got lost only three times trying to make it to Headmistress Bloodgood's office. The hallways kept shifting, leading them farther away from their destination and closer to the catacombs underneath the school.

"Not where I need to go!" Frankie groaned as yet another set of stairs moved under their feet, pulling them away from the hallway that led to Headmistress Bloodgood's office. "Where's a cartographer's temporal lobe when you need it?"

Watzie tugged on Frankie's shoelaces, still untied from their attempt at channeling a Paris fashion model, dragging them in the correct direction.

As Frankie made their way through the school-turned-labyrinth, they noticed several students glued to their iCoffins. Not literally, of course, but their gazes were fixed on an EekTok video. Frankie lowered their head as they walked, wondering if everyone was still watching the keytar post Toralei had made.

Upon finally arriving at the headmistress's office, Frankie clutched the file containing all the information about their brain parts to their chest.

"Ah, Frankie Stein!" Headmistress Bloodgood exclaimed when Frankie entered the office. The headmistress got up from her desk and walked across the room, tripping on a tile on the floor that suddenly popped up. She stumbled and, for a moment, her head detached from her neck and shot up in the air. Headmistress Bloodgood grabbed her head by the ears and quickly secured it back in place.

"My goodness, this floor! I don't recall it being so uneven yesterday," she said, motioning Frankie to a chair in front of her desk as her ax-shaped earrings swung back and forth.

"Structural integrity will often decline under eroding foundation conditions," Frankie blurted out, a small electric spark coming from their neck.

Headmistress Bloodgood nodded. "Well, let's hope it doesn't change anymore. I've already stubbed my toe three times."

Setting an iBall on her desk, Headmistress Bloodgood tapped it a few times. A static screen quickly changed and projected two faces in front of Frankie.

"Mom! Dad!" Frankie exclaimed, waving so enthusiastically at their parents that their hand popped off and fell on the floor. Grabbing the hand before it could scurry after Watzie, who was sitting at Frankie's feet, Frankie quickly reattached it to their wrist and wiggled their fingers.

"Hi, Frankie!" Dr. Victor Stein said. Even though he was smiling, his face looked serious.

"Hey there, Frankie," Dr. Mary Stein added, waving not as excitedly as she usually did when she talked to Frankie. Frankie couldn't help but notice they were calling them by their name and not an electricity-based term of endearment like they usually did.

Headmistress Bloodgood cleared her throat. "Your parents needed to speak to you. They sent me something of importance that I'm supposed to give you."

At that moment, the pipes behind the walls of Headmistress Bloodgood's office groaned and whined. The grate on the floor clattered as a madre de aguas, a Cuban sea serpent, burst through. Slithering toward the desk, the serpent spit a file out of its mouth and into the headmistress' hands. The madre de aguas retreated quickly back down the drain in the floor, leaving a trail of water in its path.

Frankie processed what was happening, their brain buzzing. A meeting in the headmistress's office. Their parents acting more serious than usual. Some mysterious item they were supposed to receive. Analyzing the evidence, Frankie knew there could be only one possible conclusion.

Something was wrong.

They grabbed the sides of their chair as Watzie snuggled against Frankie's leg. He could always sense when their circuits got overwhelmed.

"Now, there's nothing to worry about," Frankie's mom said. "We've just come across some new information regarding one of your brain parts."

For a moment, an electric pulse shot up Frankie's spine. This could be the solution to their talent show problem! Maybe this new information would help them find a new routine to do.

Frankie's dad pursed his lips. "There's been a bit of a scandal."

Frankie sighed, and their shoulders sank. Maybe not.

Headmistress Bloodgood dried the file off with a handkerchief and slid it across her desk to Frankie. Opening it, Frankie saw a picture of a woman with stringy black hair and pale skin. Squinting at the picture, Frankie noticed small green lines stretching across the woman's cheeks. They looked a lot like the veins on a plant leaf. *Dr. Valeria Hemlock, botanist,* was written at the top of the paper the photo was clipped to.

"Zaps! A botanist!" Frankie exclaimed. "How cool!"

Frankie's mom nodded, the projection from the iBall momentarily pixelating as Headmistress Bloodgood's desk shook. The headmistress placed both of her hands on the desk as her eyebrow raised.

"Yes, it is cool," Frankie's mom said. "But new information about Dr. Hemlock has been discovered. And, well, it's not great."

Frankie knit their eyebrows together, concentrating on what their mom said.

"What your mom means is that people are claiming Dr. Hemlock did unethical experiments in her laboratory," Frankie's dad said.

"Oh, I'm sure it was just a misunderstanding," Frankie said, their foot tapping on the floor. "But what did she do?"

"I think I can help explain," Headmistress Bloodgood said, taking out her iCoffin and pulling up EekTok. "Cleo DeNile showed this to me yesterday. She says it's important that I stay informed of trending topics. I'm not so sure about that, but this story is relevant."

Clicking on a video from the *Gory Gazette* newspaper, Frankie watched as a monster with a baseball cap pulled low on his forehead rubbed his chin and spat on the ground. His eyes were shadowed, but Frankie could still tell that his pupils were in slits, just like a snake. "Yes, sir, I heard it all. That woman in there would lure humans into her laboratory. And this is the honest truth—they never came back out!"

The monster continued, waving his fingers in the air. His nails were long and tinged green. "Mysteriously disappeared, they all say. Who knows what she really did to them? But no one ever saw them again."

Frankie looked past the monster as he continued speaking about Dr. Hemlock and what he thought she was doing in her lab. He stood in front of an old building covered with vines and overgrown plants. At the entrance to the building sat a large statue barely visible beneath the ivy growing all over the stone.

Watzie hopped up on Frankie's lap. Frankie wrapped their arms around his soft fur, trying to keep electric sparks from shooting from their ears as the video continued. Monster after monster speculated in an increasingly horrifying manner about what Dr. Hemlock had done to the people and monsters she brought into her lab. One werebear swore she heard screams coming from the basement in the middle of the night. The Gory Gazette even disguised themselves and interviewed a human who declared that his next-door neighbor had disappeared, last seen walking in front of Dr. Hemlock's building nestled in the middle of the town closest to Monster High.

When the video finally ended, Frankie said in a quiet voice, "This is who part of my brain part comes from?"

Headmistress Bloodgood rested her chin on her folded hands and nodded.

Frankie's dad spoke up from the iBall call. "We weren't aware of Dr. Hemlock's history when we used part of her brain. She died a week before we created you, and a lot of information regarding her past hadn't been revealed yet. We simply thought a botanist's brain would make a lovely addition to our perfect child!"

Frankie bit their lip, thinking. "But I've looked through every single page of my brain files. I've read over all the information about the parts that make me who I am. Why wasn't Dr. Hemlock's information in there?"

Frankie's dad lowered his head. "Oh, my cute little circuit, this is a terrible reason. I was using it as a bookmark."

"You know how your dad gets really into books he's reading," Frankie's mom added with a nervous chuckle.

Frankie shook their head. "I'm gonna need more information."

Sighing, Frankie's dad explained. "I was reading this incredible book of horror stories. They were so vivid and real. I got completely lost in them. But I had to stop and work on an experiment and slid Dr. Hemlock's file between the pages to keep my place. And then a flock of baby griffins flew through an open window in the lab with their huge eagle wings and started to chew on all our files with their lion teeth. We're lucky your brain box didn't get completely gobbled up. Your mother and I got so distracted cleaning up the mess that we forgot to put the file back with the rest. I'm so sorry."

Frankie took a deep breath and absorbed all the information as it bounced around their brain. The butterflies in Frankie's stomach woke up and started to flit around, making Frankie fidget in their chair. "But why is this a story in the *Gory Gazette*? Was Dr. Hemlock a human scientist or a monster scientist?"

Frankie's mom tried to manage a small smile, but she still looked serious. "Dr. Hemlock was a monster. That's why the news is all over the monster world."

Biting their lip, Frankie considered the EekTok video. "So, people think Dr. Hemlock was a bad scientist. Is it just because of what that one monster is saying? Is it just his story?"

Frankie's mom shook her head. "Unfortunately, no. A notebook was discovered in Dr. Hemlock's lab supporting exactly what that monster said. I haven't read it, but apparently it was very . . . *descriptive* about her experiments on humans."

Watzie yelped as Frankie squeezed him tighter.

Frankie knew that sometimes monsters and humans didn't get along. That's why Monster High was protected by the Shadow of Secrecy, so that humans couldn't find it. There was even a Glawackus statue at the entrance gates that would make any human who managed to find the school forget everything they had seen. Monsters needed a safe space from humans, a place where they could feel like they belonged and fit in when the world often made them feel like outsiders. But all the information about Dr. Hemlock seemed to suggest that humans needed to be safe from monsters, too. That couldn't be possible. Could it?

Before Frankie could respond, before they could ask their parents more questions about Dr. Hemlock, Headmistress Bloodgood's office began to shake uncontrollably. The iBall rolled off the desk and crashed to the floor, disconnecting the call with Frankie's parents.

"My goodness!" the headmistress exclaimed, jumping up so quickly her head spun completely around.

The windows rattled, and books slid off the shelves behind the large desk and onto the floor. The delivery dragon resting in the corner woke up and flew out the window.

"Frankie, I would love to discuss this with you further, but it seems I have more pressing matters at hand," Headmistress Bloodgood said, handing the file containing all the information about Dr. Valeria Hemlock to Frankie.

Frankie thanked the headmistress and grabbed the file, stuffing it in the middle of their already stuffed box of papers, ensuring no one would see it. They shuffled out of the office with Watzie, passing Heath, his eyes fixed on his phone, an EekTok video playing.

The same EekTok video that Frankie had just seen in the headmistress's office.

It was then that Frankie realized why all the students had been looking at their phones all day. The students of Monster High hadn't been watching Toralei's video about their keytar playing. Everyone had been watching the *Gory Gazette* video.

"Do you really think she did all those things to humans?" Lagoona asked Toralei as they stood in front of their coffin-shaped lockers.

Toralei shrugged. "The humans probably deserved it."

Spectra shot out of the wall next to Frankie and they jumped. "AHHHH!" Spectra yelled.

"Not right now, please," Frankie said in a low voice as they quickened their pace.

Spectra groaned. "No one wants to be scared today. All everyone's talking about is that bad scientist."

"Of course they are," Cleo said, flipping her hair over her shoulder as flying scarabs held her iCoffin up so she could see herself on-screen. "A monster getting caught doing experiments on humans is huge news. It's totally trending right now. I mean, monsters usually stay away from the human world. Our own school has a Shadow of Secrecy to keep humans out. Our worlds don't usually mix. Clawdeen's kind of a special case with her human dad and werewolf mom. But oh my Ra, I wish we had more of the human world here. It's loads of fun."

Frankie gripped their files tighter as they hurried back to their dorm, determined that no one would find out about Frankie's brain part. No one could know that it came from the infamous Dr. Valeria Hemlock.

CHAPTER 5

Later that evening, Frankie sat on the floor next to their bed. They'd read over the file about Dr. Hemlock seventy-three times—even though they'd memorized every word after reading it just once.

The file said that Dr. Hemlock was born in Peru. Frankie wondered what Peru was like and looked up photographs of the country on their iCoffin. Steep, green mountains popped up on the screen. There was even a mountain that looked like it had been painted with bright, colorful stripes.

An electric spark shot from Frankie's neck and their eyes turned white. In their mind, they saw a hand grip a brush and spread bright green paint across a blank canvas in a thick layer. As if they were the one painting, Frankie watched as the hand added sunny yellow circles and thin orange lines on top of the green paint.

"Are you planning a trip?" Clawdeen asked as she came into the dorm room and flopped down on her bed. "That looks like the Rainbow Mountain in Peru."

Frankie snapped out of their vision. "Zaps! My poltergeist artist brain part got me distracted," they said to themselves. Clicking off their screen, they shoved their iCoffin in their lap. "Nope," Frankie answered Clawdeen. "Staying right here at Monster High."

"Oh good," Draculaura said, flying into the room in her bat form. A pink cloud burst in the air, and she transformed back into her monster form. Draculaura sat down at the vanity next to her coffin bed and began brushing her long black hair, not phased at all by the lack of a reflection in the vanity mirror. "I wouldn't want you to miss the talent show!"

Clawdeen took out her iCoffin from her back pocket. "Did either of you see that *Gory Gazette* Eek-Tok about the evil scientist? Talk about a breaking news disaster."

Draculaura nodded, setting her hairbrush on her vanity. "I did! It's all anyone is talking about today. I heard that the doctor's notebooks were full of explanations about the terrible experiments she did on humans."

Frankie drummed their fingers on the floor. The space between two of the stones on the floor cracked open, and a small green weed shot up and wrapped itself around Frankie's index finger.

"Zaps!" Frankie exclaimed, sending an electric spark from the tip of their finger and making the weed release its hold.

Watzie barked at the weed, and it retreated into the floor. Draculaura and Clawdeen were too engrossed in their conversation about Dr. Hemlock to notice.

Clawdeen looked at Frankie. Frankie stared back, realizing that they'd missed something Clawdeen had said.

"Repeat, please," Frankie said, their fingers playing with the edge of their Monster High jacket nervously.

Clawdeen smiled. "I was just saying that it was funny you were looking at photos of Peru when that's where the *Gory Gazette* said Dr. Hemlock was from. Not 'funny ha-ha,' more like 'funny oh my gosh that scientist totally scares me.'"

"That is a very interesting coincidence that those two things would happen at the same time," Frankie said, nudging their brain part file farther under their bed.

"Oh, South America has some absolutely fantastic monsters," Draculaura said, sitting down next to Frankie and fanning her hair out over her shoulders.

"Really? Like who?" Clawdeen asked.

Draculaura bit her lip and thought for a moment. "Well, since he's Premier First and Foremost Top monster, Dad had me learn them all. They're amazing. Let's see, there's the chullachaqui. They can look like absolutely anyone they want. And then the tunche, which whistles when something bad is going to happen."

"Like a warning system?" Clawdeen asked, dangling her legs off the edge of her bed.

Draculaura nodded, and Frankie stared at her, taking in all the information.

Counting on her fingers, Draculaura finally said, "And then there's the sachamama."

A spark shot out from Frankie's neck and hit Draculaura in the shoulder.

"Oh wow! That tickled, Frankie. Were you trying to curl my hair?" Draculaura laughed.

"Sorry! Just a little excited," Frankie said. They couldn't stop their foot from tapping on the floor and wrapped their hands around their calf.

Draculaura waved her hand. "Anyway, as I was saying, the sachamama. That means 'mother of the earth.' They're shaped like a snake, and all kinds of trees and plants grow on their back."

"Oh, that's clawsome," Clawdeen said. "Can you imagine having all those plants with you all the time? Like, hey, I'm hungry. Good thing there's a screamberry bush growing right on my shoulder."

Draculaura chuckled, but Frankie didn't say anything.

"It would sit very still in the forest and open its mouth, making it look like a hole in a tree trunk," Draculaura continued, waving her hands in the air.

"Unsuspecting animals would venture into the not-tree trunk and when they did—wham!"

Draculaura slapped her hands together, making Clawdeen and Frankie jump.

"The sachamama would eat them," Draculaura said.

Clawdeen laughed and shrugged her shoulders. "A creature's gotta eat, right?"

Frankie thought for a moment. A faint electric spark traveled from their ear and tickled the corner of their blue eye and bounced to their green eye. There was one word at the bottom of Dr. Hemlock's file that kept sliding across Frankie's brain, one word that they couldn't forget.

Because it was the one word that said what kind of monster Dr. Hemlock was.

A sachamama.

Watzie nudged Frankie's leg with his nose.

"Do you think sachamamas are good or bad?" they finally said, swallowing hard to keep their voice from shaking.

Draculaura shrugged. "Well, there are no bad monsters. But there have been lots of rumors about sachamamas over the years. Mostly made up by humans trying to keep people out of the forest. You know how human parents use stories about monsters. Like 'don't stay out too late or the boogeyman will snatch you up.' As if Twyla would ever do anything like that."

"Exactly," Clawdeen huffed and rolled her eyes.

"But the rumors are that sachamamas don't only eat animals but have a taste for humans, too. And sometimes, when rumors are strong enough, you gotta wonder if they might actually be true," Draculaura said, crossing her arms.

Watzie crawled under Frankie's bed and pushed their brain file out from under the frame with his paw.

Frankie slapped their hand down over the file to keep it from moving farther and sent a spark flying across the room.

"Are you OK, Frankie?" Clawdeen asked. She tapped her long nail distractedly on her mooncclaw necklace.

Frankie couldn't help it. If they kept their secret any longer, they felt like their brain would short-circuit. The butterflies in their stomach might actually swirl up their throat and fly out of their mouth. Frankie shook their head and flipped open the file to the page about Dr. Hemlock.

"Hey, that's the scientist everyone is talking about," Clawdeen exclaimed. She leaned forward and pushed her glasses up the bridge of her nose to get a closer look at the papers.

"Why do you have a file about her?" Draculaura asked as she got up from her chair and sat next to Frankie.

Frankie tapped their finger on Dr. Hemlock's photo. "I have files with information about all the parts of my brain and who they came from," Frankie said, their voice shaking slightly.

Clawdeen hopped off her bed and sat in front of Frankie. "Wait, so does that mean . . ."

Frankie dragged their finger down the page about Dr. Hemlock. They passed a paragraph about the doctor's work combining plant, animal, and monster DNA, making improvements in each species. Reading that had made Frankie happy at first. But then they pointed to one word at the bottom—*sachamama*.

"Dr. Hemlock was a sachamama. You said that sachamamas lured animals into their mouths to eat them, maybe even humans, too. Like how they're saying Dr. Hemlock lured humans into her lab. So, I have a brain part from someone who . . . did all that."

Draculaura and Clawdeen stared at Frankie, taking in everything they said.

Frankie looked to both of their friends as Watzie snuggled next to their thigh. "So, is that bad?" they asked. "Everyone is saying the doctor was this bad monster and now she's a part of me. Does that make me bad, too?"

Draculaura sighed and put her hand on Frankie's knee. "I think you are Frankie, no matter what parts you have. And you're our friend."

Clawdeen nodded. "Exactly. It doesn't matter where your parts came from. You're still the best Frankie ever."

Frankie smiled, the electrified butterflies in their stomach settling.

Draculaura cleared her throat and scooted closer to her friend. "But, Frankie. Maybe it would be best to keep this information just between the three of us for now. Rumors have a way of getting completely out of control, and some people might not understand all the information."

Frankie's stomach butterflies took off again. Sparks flew across their brain, taking in what Draculaura said, extrapolating the variables, and concluding that if the students at Monster High found out they had a brain part from a bad monster, they would think Frankie was a bad monster, too.

No one could find out.

But it was too late.

As Toralei walked away from Frankie's dorm room, she laughed to herself, her fingers already flying over her iCoffin.

"Those three really need to learn to shut the door if they're gonna tell secrets like that."

CHAPTER 6

❅ 💀 ❅

The next day, Frankie sat with Draculaura at the casketball court while they watched Clawdeen practice.

"Oh, check it out! Skeleton dunk!" Clawdeen cried as she jumped in the air and smashed the ball through the hole in the coffin at the end of the court.

But as she started to dribble the ball again, the ground under Clawdeen's feet shook, making the ball fly wildly across the court and slam into Frankie's shoe. Frankie's combat boot, complete with foot, detached from their ankle and smacked Draculaura in the knee.

"Oh, zaps!" Frankie exclaimed, scrambling to collect their foot.

"Oh my gosh, I'm so sorry," Clawdeen said, running over to Draculaura and Frankie.

Draculaura rubbed her knee and smiled. "Well, I think my reflexes are still good."

Frankie grabbed their foot and secured it back to their ankle. "Was thinking about trying a new bionic foot I developed that lets me jump ten feet in the air. Should've tried it today!"

The trio laughed as they sat on the rocks lining the casketball court.

"Hopefully there won't be a full-on earthquake when I do my routine for the talent show. Like, I didn't exactly sign up for a free throw tremor challenge, you know," Clawdeen said. As if on cue, the rocks they were sitting on trembled.

"Something's going on," Draculaura said. "I mean, Monster High is always Monster High. You never know what to expect. But yesterday I tried to go to my clawculus class, and when I went through the classroom door, I was in the hallway leading to the catacombs! I've never been late to class before. It was awful."

Frankie nodded. "A vine popped out of the floor of the library this morning and wrapped around my ankle. I had to zap it with my finger. That botanist brain should've been useful."

Frankie's mouth slammed shut and they looked from Clawdeen to Draculaura.

"Oops," they said. "Not supposed to mention her, I guess. You know. The doctor."

Clawdeen and Draculaura nodded. Before they could say anything, their iCoffins buzzed.

"A new EekTok from Toralei?" Clawdeen asked, scrolling through her phone. "This is probably gonna be as good as finding one of Kuma's hairs in your eyescream."

Draculaura pressed play on a video as Frankie leaned against her shoulder.

Toralei stood in a hallway, waving at the camera.

"Hey there, Monster High. Toralei here with the biggest news since Heath hypnotized the creepateria cooks into serving eyescream for an entire week. But this news is a little more . . . dangerous. We've all seen the *Gory Gazette* video about Dr. Hemlock. But did you know that Dr. Hemlock was a sachamama?"

Toralei paused and stared at the camera for full effect. "For those of you not in the know, sachamamas are terrifying monsters who gobble up humans—and maybe even monsters—while they're disguised as trees."

With a smirk on her face, she continued. "And, heads up, Monster High. There might be a sachamama just like Dr. Hemlock right here in our school. Who do you think it is?"

Her eyebrow raising to a sharp point, Toralei ended her video with a statement that made Frankie's foot tap uncontrollably.

"I'll drop one clue about the sachamama's identity each day before a big reveal at the talent show!"

When the video ended, Clawdeen gripped her casketball so tightly, her claws punctured the rubber and deflated the ball. "Oh, I'm so mad I could . . . I could . . . ugh! My brain is a hyperactive pack of pups."

"That doesn't sound like a good environment for a brain to survive in," Frankie said.

"I think somehow she knows it's you, Frankie. Doesn't she?" Draculaura said, scrolling through the comments on Toralei's video. The views just kept increasing along with the comments as everyone dropped names of who they thought the sachamama at Monster High could be.

Frankie nodded. Smoothing their hand over the white streak in their hair, they said, "But don't you think it's OK? You said there were no bad monsters. So I just gotta prove to everyone that sachamamas aren't bad. Just like Toralei isn't really bad. She's not lying about there being a sachamama at Monster High, right?"

Clawdeen huffed. "Oh, we're gonna have to agree to disagree on that one, Frankie."

The ground underneath the trio shook hard enough this time to knock Draculaura off the rock she was sitting on. As Frankie helped her up, Draculaura brushed herself off and looked at Clawdeen and Frankie.

"I think a day like today calls for the Coffin Bean, don't you?" she said, straightening her skirt and fixing her hair.

Clawdeen and Frankie nodded and followed Draculaura away from the casketball court.

When they got to the Coffin Bean, though, the atmosphere was hardly relaxing. Everyone was buzzing, and not just from the caffeine-filled drinks but from Toralei's video.

"Who do you think it is?" Heath asked, touching the side of Cleo's Sar-coffee-gus and heating it up after the drink had sat too long and cooled.

Cleo raised an eyebrow, a scarab flying from under her gold armband and sticking its tongue out at Heath. She looked at Lagoona, who was sitting next to her. "Are you sure it isn't you?"

Lagoona nudged Cleo with her shoulder. "Ay, did you leave your brain in a jar? There's no way it could be me and you know it."

Draculaura ordered three zappaccinos, and they settled around a table, listening in on their classmates' conversations.

"They're not gonna know it's you, Frankie," Clawdeen whispered. "They're too busy making up rumors about each other."

At just that moment, Heath hopped up on his chair and put his hands on his hips. "Now we've all heard stories about sachamamas. Everybody's cousin's sister's chimera has some story about wandering into a forest, sitting down next to a tree, and suddenly finding that the tree tried to eat them. And now there's one of these monsters at Monster High!"

Frankie's blue and green eyes widened. "Is that true?"

Draculaura nodded. "Stories and rumors about sachamamas are pretty common, unfortunately. Dad had to form a whole committee one time to clean up the rumors about them and figure out what they were really like. But sachamamas are so rare and like to keep to themselves, so they couldn't find any to speak to the committee. The rumors kind of ended up winning."

Heath straightened his arms out and rocked side to side, the flames on his head growing. "But I think I know who it is! Ghoulia Yelps is actually a reanimated sachamama!"

Ghoulia let out a loud laugh and stuck out her tongue at Heath. "One hundred percent zombie here.

I only battle sachamamas in video games. I'm not actually one, Heath."

Heath pursed his lips as the flames in his hair grew and his eyes narrowed at the other students in the Coffin Bean. "Well, what about you, Deuce? How do we know you aren't really the sachamama?"

Wrath curled out from underneath Deuce's hat and hissed, "Liesss."

Deuce smirked and took a long sip of his chocolate milksnake. He pointed to the snake. "What he said."

Frankie gripped their cup tighter. "Sure would be nice if he would stop doing this so we could drink our beverages in peace."

"Just give up," Clawdeen called to Heath, tapping her claws on her zappaccino.

Heath hopped down from his chair. Instead of stopping his guessing game, he focused his attention on Clawdeen, Draculaura, and Frankie seated at their table.

His eyes flashed orange as he stared at Draculaura. "I don't think it's you. You don't really have a sacha-mama vibe."

Draculaura flipped her hair over her shoulder. "Correct. Game over. Now go sit down."

Clawdeen let out a nervous chuckle. "I mean, c'mon, would it really be that bad to have a sachamama at Monster High? We've got all kinds of monsters here."

Heath put his hands on his hips. "But what do we know about sachamamas? They're so rare and keep to themselves. There's no telling what they might really be like. And if it's true they're a monster that goes after *other* monsters? Better safe than served up on a sachamama platter!"

Cleo drummed her painted nails on the side of her cup. "Remember when Kuma first got here? No one knew anything about yōkai. All that roaring and throwing rocks made him seem like a pretty terrifying monster. Who knows what's rumor and what's truth with sachamamas?"

Lagoona's eyes widened. "Exactly! I'm a sea monster. What if this sachamama decides I'm a salty treat?"

Lagoona seemed to have missed Cleo's point— Kuma turned out to be more teddy bear than terrifying—but all their classmates rumbled in fearful agreement.

"I have to look out for every tree around the cemetery now," Ghoulia said, nervously tucking a strand of her blue hair under her gray beanie and adjusting her pink glasses. "What if they're really just a sachamama in hiding?"

"I heard that sachamamas are really good at blending into the human world," Spectra Vondergeist said, popping up from the floor of the Coffin Bean. "Like they can hide all the plants growing on their back, their huge unlocking jaw, and their serpent scales. They can look just like regular humans. There's no way of knowing who might be one!"

Frankie couldn't stomach another sip of their zappaccino as everyone at the Coffin Bean speculated about what having a sachamama at Monster High would really mean. And none of it was good. Even Skelita Calaveras, who always saw the positive in everything, was afraid that a sachamama would devour all the flowers she loved so much.

As speculation flew around the room, Draculaura warned Heath to stop working everyone up. Heath only sauntered closer to Frankie's table, a smirk on his face.

"Oh, I'm just guessing for fun," he said. Heath faced Frankie and narrowed his eyes. Looking them up and down, he waved his hand playfully. "Like, why couldn't Frankie here be the sachamama? I mean, do we really know where all your parts came from?"

"Rude," Clawdeen said, slamming her drink down on the table.

"Well, yes, we do know where all my parts came from," Frankie said, their brain filled with every kind of information *except* the ability to lie. "They're all listed in my files."

"But there's no sachamama listed, so problem solved!" Clawdeen jumped in loudly.

Frankie looked at Clawdeen and realized what they had said.

"But, uh," Frankie stood up and backed away from the table. "Right. My files have all the information."

Heath walked toward Frankie, chuckling. "You look a little nervous there, Frankie. Everything OK?"

"Everything is fine," Frankie said, but an electric spark shot from their elbow and up to their ear, making their head twitch.

All Frankie could do was run. Run away from Heath's prying eyes, away from the Coffin Bean, and away from all the students who would surely hate them if they found out who Frankie's brain part really came from.

CHAPTER 7

❧ 💀 ❧

Frankie ran through the trees surrounding the Coffin Bean. They ran as fast as their bionic leg would carry them.

Which was pretty fast.

Frankie couldn't lie about their brain part coming from Dr. Hemlock. Clawdeen had saved them by saying that their brain file didn't have anything about a sachamama. Did that mean this part of the real Frankie was shameful and meant to be covered up?

How could that be true if there were no bad monsters?

Frankie's brain hurt as all their parts argued with one another.

They sped over rocks and hills, but their mind was so preoccupied that they missed a tree root pushing out of the ground. Frankie's foot caught on it, and they slammed into a tree trunk. Their arms and legs detached from their torso and flew through the air, scattering on the ground.

Before they could shout zaps, their blue and green eyes lit up as electric sparks crept from their ears and across their scalp.

A new world appeared in Frankie's vision.

A steep mountain covered in green. Birds roosting in the trees squawked and flew away as Frankie grew closer.

But was it Frankie?

Or perhaps something else slithering between the tall trees stretching skyward on the mountain. Out of the corner of their vision, Frankie saw a tail twitch. They looked down at their body, their bluish gray skin replaced with dark green scales.

Frankie was a serpent!

Frankie's gaze wound its way through the forest, searching and seeking. The snake was on the move. At the base of a low hill, the creature eased itself between two large rocks. Its mouth stretched open, impossibly large, fangs stretching into branches and scales turning to bark.

And then it waited.

The snake looked up, and Frankie watched as lightning flashed overhead. The clouds grew dark and swirled above. Rain began to fall from the sky, lightly at first, and then in thick sheets, drenching the forest floor.

But the snake didn't move. It didn't close its mouth. It lay perfectly still and waited.

Quick footsteps and heavy breathing were almost drowned out by the sound of the rain pouring down. A figure in soaked clothes crawled over rocks, clutched desperately at bushes for leverage, and pushed himself off tree trunks, racing up the hill. The man's eyes darted left and right, searching for any sign of shelter from the growing storm.

As wind swirled through the forest, pushing rain in the man's face, he finally saw it.

A hollowed-out tree trunk. A safe space. A refuge from the rain.

The man raced toward the tree, moving closer and closer to Frankie, who was trapped inside the snake's perspective. They wanted to scream, to warn the man of what the tree really was. But they were held hostage by their vision, forced only to watch.

Chest heaving and out of breath, the man crept inside the dark hole in the tree trunk and out of the pounding rain. Suddenly, the rough brown bark turned to smooth green scales. Long fangs shot out from the edge of the hole.

Before Frankie could say anything, before they could scream, they looked down and watched as the tree transformed back into a serpent and snapped its mouth shut.

"Zaps!" Frankie finally exclaimed, coming out of their vision.

Slowly collecting their arms and legs and getting up from the ground, Frankie shook their head. "That can't be Dr. Hemlock," they said, swallowing hard. "That can't be me."

Their heart beat so hard, Frankie thought it might burst from their chest. They ran and ran, away from the tree that caused their vision, until they heard voices.

"Oh, great spirits, we call on you now," someone said, their voice filling the night air.

Frankie crouched behind a rock, catching their breath, and listened.

"Let us speak to those beyond the veil, to those who have passed on," the voice continued.

Peeking out from behind their rock hiding place, Frankie gasped.

Humans!

In their panic, Frankie must have run past the border of Monster High and through the Shadow of Secrecy, ending up in the woods that surrounded the school.

Three humans sat in a circle around several lit candles. They looked older than Frankie but younger than Headmistress Bloodgood. But Frankie admitted to themself that they were terrible at guessing ages, since they were only a month old.

"Who are these humans trying to talk to?" Frankie whispered to themself.

The tallest human, wearing a thick dark green coat and gray gloves with the fingertips cut off, cleared his throat.

"We call on you to speak to us, V. H.!" he called.

Frankie's eyes widened, and their fingers dug into the rock they were crouched behind. Who was V. H.?

And then Frankie's mouth dropped open. Could V. H. possibly be Valeria Hemlock? What were these humans doing trying to talk to Dr. Hemlock? How did they even know about her?

The shortest of the humans mumbled something, and Frankie strained to hear. They reached up and popped off their right ear. As quietly as possible, they tossed it closer to the humans. It landed in the grass with a soft thud, but none of the humans seemed to notice.

"We want to speak to V. H.," the short human said, her blond hair tied in two long braids that fell over her shoulders. "We want to know about your work. How could you leave the last one unfinished?"

The breeze picked up in the woods, shaking the leaves in the trees above Frankie and rustling a stack of papers next to the third human. Frankie squinted, trying to make out what the papers said, but they were too far away.

"Easy fix for that," Frankie whispered. They smacked the back of their head with their palm and popped out their left eye. They rolled the green eye through the grass and toward the papers.

"That's better," Frankie thought, and read what was written on the papers next to the third human.

"One final experiment, one final try to achieve my goal," the doctor thought as they stood over the human strapped to the table.

"You can't do this!" the human cried, struggling against the vines that held them secured to the cold metal. The vines grew and tightened around the human's body.

"Oh, but I can," said the doctor. "Because you won't even remember what I've done. You won't even recall that I ever existed."

The doctor approached the human
with a long needle, and their eyes
narrowed. "Now this won't hurt a
bit." The doctor smirked. "Well,
maybe just a little sting."

Frankie covered their mouth to keep from scream-
ing. How did these humans have Dr. Hemlock's journals? Headmistress Bloodgood mentioned that the
doctor's journals had been discovered, outlining all
of her experiments on humans. This must be exactly
what the headmistress was talking about.

With an electric zap, Frankie summoned their ear
that was listening to the humans and their eye that
had read from Dr. Hemlock's journal and popped
them back into place. Pushing themself off the rock,
Frankie ran away from the humans. The farther they
could get from this séance trying to contact the doctor, the better.

Frankie had to get back to Monster High. They had
been afraid this whole time that sachamamas might
be bad and that Dr. Hemlock might actually be an
evil scientist.

Now they were afraid they might have the answer. And it wasn't the one Frankie wanted.

Frankie raced over the hills and past the trees that led toward Monster High. They burst through the Shadow of Secrecy and slammed directly into the Glawackus statue that stood at the entrance to the school. Luckily, this time all their limbs stayed in place.

Looking up from the ground where they lay out of breath, Frankie stared at the statue. It was a lion sculpture based on a monster with a hyena-like cackle. His purpose at Monster High was to erase the memories of humans who mistakenly stumbled upon the school.

And his sculpture looked familiar.

Frankie searched their brain for a memory, for evidence of something they knew they had seen.

Jumping up from the ground, Frankie hit upon the right memory and gasped. "Zaps!"

The ivy-covered statue in front of the building that contained Dr. Hemlock's laboratory looked exactly like the Glawackus statue at the entrance of Monster High.

Frankie rubbed their temples. Too many thoughts were bouncing around their brain parts.

"What could this possibly mean?" Frankie mumbled, shuffling back to a school they weren't certain would welcome them if everyone knew the truth.

CHAPTER 8

F rankie made their way back into Monster High, hoping they didn't run into any other students— and wishing their brain would stop replaying the vision of the sachamama. They kept seeing it in a constant loop, along with the words from Dr. Hemlock's notebook.

Not ready to face Clawdeen and Draculaura, Frankie meandered past the library. A door with a large sign reading COME IN! popped up in the hallway. The long wooden slats on the floor shifted, sliding Frankie toward the door.

"No, thank you," Frankie said, pushing themself away from the door. "That's not where I want to go right now."

Frankie found a quiet corner near the entrance to the classroom wing of Monster High and sat down under a long set of stairs.

"Was Dr. Hemlock really an evil scientist? Are sachamamas really bad monsters?" Frankie asked themself. They wished they could run to Manny in the library and ask to see a chart or diagram that would explain everything.

The stones in the wall Frankie was leaning against shifted as Monster High shook. A small green vine grew out of the wall and wrapped around Frankie's ankle.

Frankie touched the vine lightly with their finger and gave the vine a small zap. For a moment, the vine went from green to light brown, and then it disappeared back into the wall.

Narrowing their eyes, Frankie investigated the wall.

"I'd be careful sitting under the stairs."

Frankie jumped.

Cleo came around the corner and gave Frankie a small smile. "Monster High has been shaking enough these days. You're taking a big risk being under there. Like, 'get smooshed by shifting stairs and walls' risk."

Frankie stood up and brushed their hands on their black jeans. "Thanks," they said.

Frankie walked around to the bottom of the stairs and sat down on the last step.

Cleo crossed her arms and looked Frankie up and down. The butterflies in Frankie's stomach started to flit around, but Frankie wasn't sure why.

"You're not with your usual crew," Cleo said, tucking her iCoffin in her back pocket.

Frankie raised their eyebrow in confusion. "My crew?"

"Draculaura and Clawdeen."

"Oh, right," Frankie nodded. "Just needed some time by myself."

Cleo sat down next to Frankie, twirling her silky black hair between her fingers. "I get that. This place can be a lot sometimes, right?"

"The shaking walls, vines popping through the floor, and doors appearing out of nowhere are already too much," Frankie mumbled. "Never mind my new brain part."

"Your what?" Cleo asked, looking intensely at Frankie.

Waving their hand, Frankie stammered, "Oh, no. Not that. I meant all those rumors about Dr. Hemlock going around."

Cleo narrowed her eyes. "But you said your brain part. What does your brain part have to do with Dr. Hemlock?"

Frankie's fingers quivered as their foot tapped uncontrollably on the floor. Their mouth opened and shut as they tried to find the right words to say. "No, not the Dr. Hemlock rumors. Or the brain part. It's just all the talk of the sachamama at school. Yeah, that's it."

Cleo tapped a long fingernail on her red lips, thinking. She took a deep breath. "Frankie, what aren't you telling me? Do you . . . have a brain part from Dr. Hemlock?"

Frankie examined Cleo's face. Her eyes were rimmed with thick black liner, which might make her seem harsh to some people. But Frankie thought she looked really pretty. And she always told Frankie exactly what she was thinking.

Nodding slowly, Frankie said, "Yes. I do."

Frankie waited for Cleo to respond. Their heart beat faster for what seemed like minutes. The stairs shook slightly underneath them, and Frankie fidgeted.

"That's amazing!" Cleo finally exclaimed, clapping. She smiled widely at Frankie, and a small electric spark shot from Frankie's neck.

"Wait. You really think so?" Frankie asked.

Cleo nodded enthusiastically. "Of course. She was a brilliant scientist. I read up on her. She was doing amazing work making plants more resistant to disease and helping animals avoid going extinct by improving their DNA."

"And that's good, right?" Frankie asked.

Cleo slapped her leg. "Are you kidding me? Of course it is. You now have all that knowledge and power, which you can access. That's incredible."

Frankie shrugged. "Except I'm having trouble accessing my Dr. Hemlock brain part. I've seen visions from her life, but I can't get enough information to decide what she was really like. And the rumors. What about all those horrible things people are saying Dr. Hemlock did?"

Cleo crossed her arms and narrowed her eyes at Frankie. "Is Dr. Hemlock's past the same as your past?"

"I'm just a few weeks old," Frankie said.

Cleo smiled. "Exactly. Who cares what Dr. Hemlock did?"

Frankie sighed. They liked how Cleo spoke to them. It was always straightforward. Frankie never doubted what Cleo thought or felt.

"But what about the sachamama? That's what kind of monster Dr. Hemlock was, and everyone is saying that they're bad and scary."

Cleo raised an eyebrow and pursed her lips. "So prove them wrong."

"What?"

"Prove. Them. Wrong."

Frankie hopped up from the stairs and turned to Cleo. "You're saying that if I can show everyone that Dr. Hemlock wasn't an evil scientist and that sachamamas aren't bad monsters, everything will be OK?"

Cleo shrugged. "Sounds like it."

The wooden boards making up the stairs under her started to groan and come apart. The individual pieces detached from the wall, glided through the air, and formed themselves into a large arch on the opposite wall where a new door appeared with a large sign reading RIGHT HERE!

Cleo smirked and pointed to the door. "I don't suppose your amazing brain knows anything about that, does it? This whole shaking school thing is getting old."

Frankie looked at Cleo. "That's past my current limits of comprehension at the moment."

Cleo chuckled and smiled at Frankie. Holding out her hand, she said, "Don't worry, Frankie. I'll keep your secret. Locked away in a jar like my right kidney."

Frankie took Cleo's hand and shook it gently, a slight spark shooting from their palm.

Cleo giggled. "That tickled!"

As Cleo walked away, Frankie felt inspired. They had a new mission—prove that Dr. Hemlock wasn't hurting humans with her experiments and that sachamamas weren't bad monsters.

Now if only they could get the butterflies in their stomach to calm down.

Frankie marched back to their dorm room. But when they opened the door, they were met with a dark hallway instead.

Somehow, the doors had been switched.

"Not now!" Frankie shouted, slamming the door shut. "Got lots of work to do!"

When they opened the door again, everything was back to normal.

"Where'd you run off to? You should join me on the casketball court if you can run that fast," Clawdeen said, hopping up from her bed. Draculaura closed the book she was reading on her bed and sat up.

"Needed, uh, some time to think," Frankie stammered. Draculaura set her book aside. "You can tell us anything, Frankie. What's going on?"

Frankie took a deep breath and nervously rubbed the back of their neck. "I saw a vision of a sachamama. They . . . they ate a human."

Clawdeen gasped.

Draculaura took a deep breath, tapping her finger on the cover of her book. "Frankie, I'll admit there were monsters in the past who did things like that. But monsters and humans have lived peacefully for a long time by just keeping to themselves. I'm sure a monster wouldn't do that to a human."

"But I saw it! And then I went to the park outside of Monster High and saw some humans trying to call on Dr. Hemlock's ghost. They had a part of her journal, and it showed she was holding humans captive and doing horrible experiments on them." Frankie's words tumbled out in a rush and they lost their breath.

Draculaura bit her lip. "Do you really think all that is true?"

"Are you sure you saw what you think you saw?" Clawdeen asked. "Because, I mean, sometimes I think I've seen pretty strange things, but then I realize I just need to clean my glasses."

Frankie clenched their fists at their sides. "I'm not sure if it was real or not. So, I'm going to prove that

Dr. Hemlock is innocent and that sachamamas aren't bad monsters."

"How are you going to do that?" Draculaura asked.

Frankie smiled. "By going on a field trip. Want to come?"

CHAPTER 9

Are you sure this is a good idea?" Draculaura asked
as she, Clawdeen, and Frankie stepped past the
Glawackus statue and out the gates of Monster High.

Clawdeen shrugged. "Venturing into the human
world to search down Dr. Hemlock's lab and explore
it for answers? Sure, it's about as good an idea as sitting next to Goobert in the creepateria. You know your
lunch is gonna get swallowed up."

Frankie marched forward with determination.
"The cost-benefit analysis of the situation determines
that the potential benefits of the outcome outweigh
the risks."

Clawdeen looked Frankie up and down, blinking.
"You wanna run that by me again?"

Shaking their head and smiling, Frankie chuckled. "Finding out more information about Dr. Hemlock and sachamamas will be worth anything we might run into."

Frankie led the way through the trees and over the hills. They passed some burnt candles on the ground, remnants of the séance Frankie saw earlier. They searched for the pages of Dr. Hemlock's journal that the humans had, but they were gone.

"Besides, the human world isn't scary. Trust me, I would know," Clawdeen said.

Draculaura huffed. "Speak for yourself. Have you ever been chased by flaming torches and pitchforks?"

"Only by Coach Thunderbird in P.E. class," Frankie said.

Clawdeen laughed, and Draculaura transformed into a bat in a puff of smoke. "My feet hurt. This is much better."

Looking at Draculaura flying overhead, Clawdeen waved her arms. "Nope. Not here. The number of pink talking bats that humans tolerate in their world is absolutely zero."

Clawdeen had shifted to her human form and had made sure that Frankie and Draculaura blended into the world outside of Monster High as much as possible. There was only so much they could do—but bats were definitely not part of the plan.

Draculaura groaned, spun through the air, and swirled back into her monster form. "Ugh. Fine."

"So," Clawdeen said, jogging up to Frankie as they stomped through the forest. "How will we even find Dr. Hemlock's laboratory? My evil scientist lair radar is currently broken."

Frankie stopped in their tracks, their feet skidding in the dirt. Clawdeen bumped into their back as Draculaura stumbled into Clawdeen.

Sucking in a breath, Frankie closed their eyes. "In the *Gory Gazette* video, the man spreading rumors about Dr. Hemlock was standing in front of her lab. The building was covered with overgrown bushes and vines, and there looked like there was a statue in front of the building, kind of like the Glawackus statue we have at Monster High. Oh, and the street sign over his right shoulder said Main Street and Elm Avenue."

"Those are very human-sounding street names," Clawdeen said. "Not exactly getting 'building full of doom and gloom' vibes from those."

"I think I prefer Maim Street and Third Eye Avenue," Draculaura commented. "But that's incredible that you can remember all that just from the *Gory Gazette*'s EekTok video."

Frankie tapped their temple and smiled. "Photographic memory!"

The trio headed into town and meandered past coffee shops that didn't serve zappaccinos, bookstores whose books couldn't fly off the shelves all by themselves, and schools where students learned human biology instead of monster boo-ology.

Draculaura stopped in front of the window display at the bookstore, taking in a stack of books featuring dress patterns and designs.

"At least the human world has decent fashion. Not to-die-for, but . . . decent" she said.

"Look at this," Clawdeen said, pointing to a flyer taped to the inside of the window.

Frankie read the flyer. "The Bloody Brain Book Club meets every second Tuesday after a full moon to discuss the stories of great horror authors like Edgar Allan Poe, Stephen King, and our local favorite, V. H. Sachs."

Draculaura smiled. "OK, so maybe the human world isn't so bad," she said as the trio continued down the street. "But are you one hundred percent certain I can't just fly to Dr. Hemlock's lab?"

Frankie nodded. "There's no need. Because we're here."

Pointing to a small, two-story building covered with vines, Frankie walked quickly to a street sign that said Main Street and Elm Avenue. At the entrance to the building stood a large sculpture covered in ivy.

Clawdeen pushed some of the ivy aside and revealed a lion stone figure.

"It definitely is a Glawackus statue," she said. "But what would Dr. Hemlock need with a statue that can erase people's memories?"

Frankie scuffed her foot on the sidewalk and eyed every inch of the statue.

"Maybe we shouldn't jump to conclusions yet," Draculaura said.

"I'm not jumping anywhere," Frankie responded. "My feet are too tired."

Clawdeen walked cautiously up to the entrance of the building. "So do we just go in? Like we're just gonna wander into the mysterious scientist's house? Because that might make the list of top three bad ideas I've had this week."

She placed her hand on the doorknob and jiggled it. Nothing happened.

"Great. It's locked," Draculaura said. "Now what?"

Frankie squinted and spotted a partially open window at the side of the building. "Easy fix," they said, detaching their left hand. It scurried across the grass and into the window. After a minute, Frankie heard a pop at the front door, and it swung open.

"Clawsome!" Clawdeen said as Frankie's hand scampered back to their wrist and reattached itself.

"Yes, so excited that we can easily venture into the possibly evil scientist's lair," Draculaura said sarcastically.

Frankie led Draculaura and Clawdeen up the steps, through the door, and into Dr. Hemlock's lab. It was dark, and dust floated through the air.

Blinking, Frankie activated their blue and green eyes so they glowed brightly.

"That's better," Frankie said.

The room flooded with light. It was practically bare, with only a long table in the center and two bookcases along one wall. Cobwebs covered beakers and vials piled on the metal table. Draculaura took a step forward, and a crunching sound filled the air.

"Be careful," she said. "Seems like there's broken glass on the floor."

Clawdeen ran her finger along the dust covering a bookshelf in the corner. "None of these seem to be notebooks or journals. They're printed books. And wow, it looks like Dr. Hemlock had one of the biggest collections of horror novels I've ever seen. Someone was *definitely* a fan."

"Anything here activating any memories for you, Frankie?" Draculaura asked, holding up a beaker and brushing the dust off it.

Frankie looked around. They tried to imagine Dr. Hemlock sitting in her lab and working. Squeezing their fists at their sides, they grimaced. But nothing happened. Nothing shocked their brain into seeing a memory from Dr. Hemlock.

Draculaura stepped around the long metal table. "There's one thing I'm noticing," she said.

"What's that?" Clawdeen asked, tapping her finger against a dusty beaker.

"Well, we're looking at what's here in the lab. We're not paying attention to what's *not* in the lab," Draculaura answered.

"There are a lot of things that aren't here," Frankie said, scanning the spines on the bookshelf. "Goblin boogers, eyescream sandwiches, delivery dragons."

Draculaura chuckled. "Well, yes, those things. But look at all the equipment Dr. Hemlock has for her experiments. The ones she was supposedly doing on humans. What do you see?"

Frankie walked over from the bookcase and ran their finger across the metal table, picking up a trail of dust as they went. "There's lots of beakers and vials. Containers of solution. Bunsen burners to heat up liquids."

"And what *don't* you see?" Draculaura asked, crossing her arms.

"Well, it is dark in here," Clawdeen groaned.

Draculaura threw up her hands and sighed. "There aren't any scalpels or knives! Nothing that could be used to hurt someone."

Frankie bit their lip. "Do you think . . . do you think this means the experiments that Dr. Hemlock was doing weren't actually harmful to humans?"

Before anyone could answer, a voice called from outside the building. "Oh wow! The door's unlocked!"

"Do you think this is the right place?" another voice said.

A third voice piped in. "This is the statue that's on the cover of that book. It must be her place."

Clawdeen looked at Draculaura and Frankie with wide eyes. "We have to get out of here!" she whispered.

Frankie looked around and saw another door in the far corner of the room. "There!" they said, pulling Draculaura's arm as Clawdeen followed.

Footsteps followed behind them as whoever had been outside the building had gathered their courage enough to enter Dr. Hemlock's lab.

Frankie took a quick glance back as they hurried through the door and immediately recognized the three humans creeping through the entrance. It was the same ones they'd seen having a séance in the forest outside of Monster High! The humans' jaws dropped, and their eyes grew wide as they took in Dr. Hemlock's lab. One of them was wearing a black T-shirt with a logo for the Bloody Brain Book Club in the center.

Clawdeen closed the door behind them, but Frankie put their hand on her arm. "Wait, I want to know why they're here," Frankie whispered.

Crouching under a window, Frankie smacked the back of their head, and their right eye popped out into their hand. They detached their left arm and held the eye cradled in their hand above the windowsill so they could see the humans inside.

"They're looking around Dr. Hemlock's lab," Frankie said as Draculaura and Clawdeen sat in the grass with them. "But they seem really preoccupied with the books on the bookshelves. Not so much the lab equipment. I think they're from that club we saw the flyer for at the bookstore."

"Can you hear them?" Clawdeen asked.

Frankie popped off their ear and set it on the windowsill, pointed at the humans. Their eyebrows raised.

"They're talking about Dr. Hemlock!" Frankie gasped.

"What are they saying about her?" Draculaura asked.

Frankie pursed their lips. "It's muffled, but one of them is saying that the lab seems familiar. Like they've been there before."

"Do you think that's possible? I mean, we had to use your detached hand to unlock the door! No way humans could've done that," Clawdeen said.

Frankie gripped their right fist, the only one still attached to their body, at their side. "They're calling Dr. Hemlock 'Valeria.' Like they knew her. Oh zaps! She was in the Bloody Brain Book Club!"

"The one from the flyer?" Draculaura asked.

Frankie nodded. "They just said that Valeria was a reading machine, but she wasn't really made of gears, was she? Sachamamas aren't like that ."

Frankie moved away from the windowsill, re-attaching their ear and popping their eye back in its socket. They twisted their arm into their shoulder and wiggled their fingers. "I'm not sure what information about Dr. Hemlock we've really found out. This is so confusing."

Draculaura sighed, picking at the grass at her feet. "Well, this field trip has been a bust."

Frankie shook their head. "Nothing exploded."

"But all we found out is that Dr. Hemlock was possibly erasing the memories of humans because of her Glawackus statue, which may or may not be a bad thing. And we know that she was a huge fan of horror novels and was somehow in a book club for humans. I don't know what to do with that information," Draculaura said. "Now what?"

"Well, we still don't know much about the other part of Dr. Hemlock—the fact that she was a sacha-mama," Frankie said. "If only there was someone we could talk to who's a monster expert."

Clawdeen laughed and slapped Frankie on the back. "I know just the person."

CHAPTER 10

Pupster!" Mr. Wolf shouted as he opened the door.

"Hi, Dad," Clawdeen said with a chuckle as her dog, Crescent, jumped up and down and barked at her dad's feet.

"What brings my favorite daughter home from Monster High?" Mr. Wolf said as he ushered Clawdeen, Draculaura, and Frankie into the living room.

Clawdeen smirked. "I'm your only daughter."

"Statistically, the odds are definitely in your favor to be the favorite," Frankie said, sitting down on the couch with Draculaura and Clawdeen as Crescent sniffed their combat boot.

Clawdeen smiled at her dad. She'd missed living with him ever since she enrolled at Monster High, but she knew her human father was glad that his daughter could explore her werewolf side there. It made Clawdeen feel closer to her monster mom.

Mr. Wolf laughed. "Are these your friends?" he asked.

Draculaura stuck out her hand, and Mr. Wolf shook it. "Hi, I'm Draculaura," she said. "Clawdeen and I are roommates. My pronouns are she/her."

Frankie waved at Mr. Wolf and said, "I'm Frankie and I'm Clawdeen's roommate, too. My pronouns are they/them."

Mr. Wolf nodded and smiled. "Well, it's nice to finally meet you all. I've only ever met one of Clawdeen's classmates at Monster High, and that was certainly an adventure."

Frankie and Draculaura knew all about Cleo tagging along with Clawdeen on a visit home. Apparently, she'd attempted to increase her popularity by putting all the patrons of the local Egyptian restaurant under her power.

It didn't work.

"So, we're here because we need information about sachamamas," Clawdeen said. "We figured it was best to ask the world's top monster researcher."

When Clawdeen first revealed to her father that she was a werewolf, she hadn't been sure how he'd react. But Mr. Wolf had known about werewolves all along. He'd actually met Clawdeen's mom, Selena, through his monster research! And it turned out he was incredibly excited that his daughter inherited that part of her mom.

Mr. Wolf rubbed his chin and thought for a moment. "You certainly did pick a rare species of monster. Any particular reason why?"

"Well," Frankie chuckled nervously. "One of my brain parts is from a famous scientist who was a sachamama. I'm trying to find out what that means." Since Mr. Wolf was one of the rare humans who loved instead of feared monsters, they knew they could trust him.

Mr. Wolf rose from his chair and walked over to a plastic fish statue hanging on the wall. He pushed a button underneath it, and the fish's eyes glowed red.

The bookcase next to the fish moved, revealing stacks of books and gadgets.

"Oh, I could use one of those for our room," Draculaura said.

"This is all my monster research equipment. One of these books might have information about sachamamas," Mr. Wolf said, running his finger along the books. He pulled one off the shelf and sat back down.

Frankie glanced at the cover. "The Complete Encyclopedia of Monsters by Don Tella Soul?"

Mr. Wolf winked. "It has secret information that no other books have. Don was a researcher friend of mine who traveled the world interviewing monsters."

"Did he go all the way to Peru and interview sachamamas?" Draculaura asked, leaning forward.

Crescent curled up on Clawdeen's lap as Mr. Wolf opened the book and flipped through the pages.

"Let's see," Mr. Wolf said, biting his lip. "Seems like he made it to Peru but had a hard time finding sachamamas. Oh wow, he certainly found a lot of rumors about them."

Frankie groaned. "That's the problem we've been having. It seems like people know more sachamama gossip than they do actual facts about them."

Mr. Wolf nodded. "And I think monsters are very aware of the fact that not everyone separates truth from rumors."

Clawdeen scratched behind Crescent's ear. "So based on that book, is it fact or rumor that sachamamas eat humans?"

Flipping a page, Mr. Wolf took a deep breath. "Well, it says here that sachamamas can wait for days for their prey. That means they must be very patient monsters."

Frankie rubbed the back of their neck, and a spark shot from their finger and into their ear. "That's a good thing, right?"

Clawdeen nodded. "I get annoyed after waiting thirty seconds for my popcorn in the microwave. So, yes, that's good."

Mr. Wolf held out the book for Frankie to see. There was a sketch of a man with long black hair, just like

Frankie had seen on Dr. Hemlock. A flower sprouted from the back of the man's hand while leaves grew out of his shoulders.

"A sachamama can disguise themself as any plant. That seems very useful," Mr. Wolf said.

"Oh wow, can you do that, Frankie?" Dracu-laura asked.

Frankie pursed their lips and squeezed their hands into fists. They took a deep breath. But nothing happened other than a spark shooting from their knee and scaring Crescent.

"Doesn't seem like it," Frankie said.

"What are some of the rumors that your friend found? Just so we know what we're up against," Dracu-laura said.

Mr. Wolf ran his finger across the page. "It says here that some villagers swore that a sachamama flew through the air, swooped down, and stole an entire herd of pigs."

Frankie raised their eyebrows. "That seems . . . unlikely."

Mr. Wolf chuckled. "I agree. Another rumor here says that sachamamas could transform into more than just plants. They could take the form of other humans. One person swore it was a sachamama they were kissing when they thought it was their girl-friend."

Clawdeen smirked. "I think someone was just try-ing to cover up their mistake."

Mr. Wolf kept reading, and the list of sachamama rumors grew longer, each one more fantastical than the last. Because the researcher had never met one in person, all they had to rely on was other people's opinions and gossip. None of it was very encourag-ing to Frankie.

Sensing the book wasn't helping anymore, Mr. Wolf closed the book and set it on the coffee table in front of him. "Frankie, I think you need to focus on the good aspects of having part of a sachamama. That means you've got their patience and their connection to plants. And since your sachamama was a scientist, you can add all that knowledge to the list, too. What an incredible thing!"

Frankie smiled widely. "Thanks, Mr. Wolf."

Draculaura leaned over to Clawdeen and whispered in her ear, "I really like your dad."

Mr. Wolf slapped his hands on his lap and said, "Well, I hope you're staying for dinner. I can make my world-famous jambalaya!"

Frankie, Clawdeen, and Draculaura nodded enthusiastically as Crescent barked.

Over steaming bowls of jambalaya, Clawdeen told her dad all about being the reigning dodge pitchfork champion, and Draculaura explained her new fear-leading routine. Frankie zapped Mr. Wolf's bowl when his jambalaya got too cold and demonstrated their ideas for the Monster High talent show.

After dinner, Clawdeen led Frankie and Draculaura to her bedroom, where they sat and digested not only Mr. Wolf's jambalaya but everything they had learned that day. Frankie sat on the floor, resting their back on the edge of Clawdeen's bed as they scratched Crescent behind the ear.

"Brain overload today, right?" Frankie asked.

Clawdeen nodded as she flopped down on her

bed. "It's a lot to take in. If I had circuits, they'd be fried."

Spinning in a circle in the chair at Clawdeen's desk, Draculaura chuckled. "Any chance you have a super-computer brain bit that can analyze all this information for us and figure it out?"

Frankie sighed as Crescent curled up in their lap. "I think I'd like to be just Frankie for a moment."

Clawdeen rolled over and patted Frankie on the shoulder. "Is it hard to hear yourself with all those other brain parts making noise?"

Biting their lip, Frankie nodded. "Sometimes. When I have a thought, I can't help but wonder if that's me thinking or one of my brain bits."

Draculaura stopped spinning and raised her eyebrow. "But why wouldn't it be you? It's *your* brain part. That makes it you."

Clawdeen propped herself up on her elbows. "Draculaura's right. I know it's not exactly the same, but I used to wonder how to balance the human part of me with the werewolf part."

"How did you figure it out?" Frankie asked.

Clawdeen shrugged. "I realized I didn't have to. I'm one hundred percent human and one hundred percent werewolf."

"But you can't be two hundred percent of anything," Frankie said. "That's statistically impossible."

Clawdeen smiled gently at her friend. "It just means I don't need to pick a side. Instead of feeling like I'm not human enough because I'm part werewolf or not werewolf enough because I'm part human, I realized I'm exactly enough of both."

Frankie thought a moment. "So, I'm one hundred percent chupacabra architect, zombie mathematician, and human chemist."

"And sachamama botanist," Clawdeen added. "If you want to be."

"That's a lot of things to be all at once," Frankie said, smoothing down Crescent's fur with their hand.

"A lot of amazing things!" Draculaura exclaimed.

Heading back to Monster High that evening, Frankie felt better. Draculaura said she thought

Frankie was walking on air, but Frankie knew that was impossible unless they were Spectra. But focusing on the positive aspects of sachamamas made Frankie feel like they could face all the rumors at school.

And then their iCoffin buzzed in their pocket.

"Oh no," Clawdeen said, walking through the gates at Monster High. "Is that what I think it is?"

Draculaura took out her phone and nodded. The butterflies in Frankie's stomach started to swirl.

"Being able to walk on air sure doesn't last long," Frankie groaned.

Pushing through the doors of Monster High, Frankie saw all the students staring at their phones. Draculaura clicked on Toralei's latest EekTok post.

"Hey there, Monster High," Toralei purred in her video. "I promised you a clue about the sachamama we have roaming the very halls of our school, and this clue will give you a shock if you put all its pieces together. A sachamama might slither, a sachamama might wait, but Monster High's sachamama is a fellow classmate."

"There's no way anyone would connect that directly to you," Draculaura said to Frankie. "Toralei is just making it obvious that the sachamama isn't a teacher or staff member."

Frankie nodded but looked around at the main hallway in Monster High. All of the students were whispering to each other, trying to solve Toralei's riddle.

"But if Toralei keeps giving clues like this, eventually they're gonna lead to Frankie," Clawdeen said. "Because it's not so much the clue she gave but what she said right before about it giving a 'shock' and having lots of pieces. That's our Frankie."

The electricity in Frankie's brain began to buzz as their thoughts swirled together. Mr. Wolf had helped Frankie focus on the good aspects of sachamamas, but Frankie still couldn't forget the vision they'd seen in the forest of a sachamama eating a human.

They had to find out if it was true. They had to get more information about the doctor and what really happened to her.

And they needed to get it straight from the source—Dr. Hemlock herself.

While Draculaura and Clawdeen tried to distract Monster High from Toralei's EekTok by antagonizing the garbage goblins to chase after everyone's phones, Frankie hurried back to their room.

They reached under their bed for their brain file and opened it to the papers about Dr. Hemlock.

"That vision I saw in the forest can't be real," Frankie thought to themself. "It had to just be a dream because of all the rumors I heard. Clearly my subconscious flooded my cerebral cortex with dopamine and gave me a vision based on fantasy. And that journal those humans had must be fake. How would they get a hold of it anyway?"

Watzie hopped up on Frankie's bed and barked.

"Hey there, best assistant Watzie," Frankie said, ruffling the top of Watzie's head with their hand. "Just have to figure out how to get my brain to access Dr. Hemlock's memories. That'll show me what she was really doing."

Watzie barked again in agreement.

Frankie scanned the file about Dr. Hemlock. "It's frustrating having so much trouble accessing my Dr. Hemlock brain part. It's never this difficult. Usually, I'm blurting out equations in clawculus and reciting French poetry in monster arts class."

Frankie scratched absentmindedly behind Watzie's ear. "You don't think . . . well, if the doctor really was bad, maybe my brain is trying to keep me from accessing all the information she knew?"

Watzie licked Frankie's hand and sent an electric spark spiraling around their wrist. Frankie shook their head. "Well, there's only one way to find out. Maybe if I shout key words from their life, it will trigger a memory."

Standing in the middle of the room, Frankie put their hands on their hips and shouted, "Peru! Plants!"

Tapping their foot on the floor, they waited. A small spark shot from Frankie's elbows after each word, but other than that nothing happened.

Making sure the door to the dorm room was securely shut, Frankie lowered their voice and said, "Sachamama!"

Still nothing happened other than a slight spark shooting from Frankie's knee joint.

Frankie tried one more time.

"DNA!"

A large spark shot from Frankie's wrist, and Watzie barked. Frankie's fingers clenched up uncontrollably and their hand shook.

"Zaps! I short-circuited myself," Frankie said.

Heading to their closet where they kept all the bionic limbs they'd created, Frankie chuckled, "Just need to swap it out and we can keep trying, can't we, Watzie?"

Frankie scanned their limbs hanging from hooks in the closet. There was one that had a power drill instead of a palm, another with large magnetic disks on each nail, and still another that had every cooking tool imaginable in place of fingers.

"Oh, maybe this one," Frankie said. "Just made it. Would be good to try out with all these weeds that keep popping up everywhere."

Frankie grabbed a hand that had a small spade instead of a thumb and a garden trowel in place of the other four fingers. Removing their short-circuited hand with a quick twist, Frankie secured the new hand on their wrist.

The moment Frankie snapped it in place, an electric shot bolted up their spine. Their eyes flashed white as their limbs stiffened.

A fog of gray mist cleared, and Frankie found themself meandering between tall bookshelves. Row after row of books passed by until a long table appeared in front of a large window.

Frankie was in the Monster High library.

Their vision moved through the library until they were seated at the table next to a candle that cast a dim light. As they hunched over a thick book, Frankie looked down at their hands and noticed thin green lines like the veins on a plant covering their skin.

Their hands flipped through the pages of the book, but the words were fuzzy, and Frankie couldn't read them.

A group of students seated at a table near Frankie erupted into a fit of laughter as one of the students froze the book another one was reading with a single touch.

Frankie's vision looked from the students and back to their book repeatedly as they tried to go back to reading.

But three books flew off a shelf all on their own, swirled through the air, and slammed down on the table right next to Frankie. They jumped and groaned, rolling their eyes at their classmates' antics.

Gathering the book and papers and holding them to their chest, Frankie shuffled out of the library.

Frankie's vision moved through the hallways of Monster High, going up one staircase, around a corner, down another staircase. They walked the labyrinth of the school searching for a place to study. Somewhere quiet. Somewhere they could be alone.

At the end of a long hallway, Frankie's veined hand reached out to open a thick wooden door. The hinges creaked and echoed off the stone walls. Frankie peered through the doorway, another long corridor in front of them lined with lit torches. Stepping over the threshold, Frankie peeked over their shoulder one last time and caught their reflection in the large mirror hanging over the mass of potted screamthorn in the hallway.

Frankie gasped.

It was impossible not to recognize the girl's pale skin, dark eyes, and green veins, especially after Frankie had memorized every single inch of the photograph sitting in their file.

As Frankie came out of the vision, they doubled over and wrapped their arms around their waist.

"Big news, Watzie," they said, breathless. "Dr. Hemlock was a student at Monster High!"

CHAPTER 11

T he following day, Frankie stared down a pitchfork as it barreled toward their head. Just before the four sharp tines could hit Frankie, they popped their head up from their neck, and the pitchfork flew through the now-empty space and hit the wall behind Frankie.

"Zaps! That was close," Frankie said with a chuckle, securing their head back in place.

Draculaura ran over to Frankie, breathless. "Have I mentioned that dodge-pitchfork day is my least favorite day in P.E.?"

"Only about twelve times," Clawdeen said, laughing. She ducked a flying pitchfork but shot her hand up and caught it as it flew over her head. Twisting it around quickly like a baton, Clawdeen launched it at the team on the other side of the gym. "Which is only two more times than the last time we played."

"Yes, Wolf! That's it!" Coach Thunderbird shouted from the sidelines, beating her large brown wings frantically. She spoke out of the corner of her mouth, her loud whistle always perched in her beak, ready to blast a shrill sound through the gym.

Another pitchfork sailed toward Frankie, but they were too busy watching Cleo fix her shiny black hair into a high ponytail, and they missed dodging it. The pitchfork slammed into their calf, detaching their bionic leg right below the knee and pinning it to the wall behind them.

"Walk it off, Stein," Coach Thunderbird called. "It's just a mild impaling."

Frankie hopped over to where the pitchfork held their leg and yanked it out of the wood paneling. Reattaching their leg, they turned to run back to Draculaura and Clawdeen but slammed into Toralei's back instead as she dodged a pitchfork.

Frankie and Toralei fell to the ground in a tangle of limbs.

"Zaps!" Frankie said. "Sorry about that."

Toralei hissed but then took a deep breath when she saw Frankie. She blew her bangs off her forehead with a smirk. "Oh my, that's OK, Frankie. Or should I call you Dr. Hemlock?"

"Well, no you shouldn't, because that's not my name," Frankie said, shaking their head. And then they realized what Toralei actually meant. "Oh."

Toralei stood up and brushed her hands on her knees. "I think it might be time for an EekTok update, don't you?"

Before Frankie could answer, Toralei skipped over to Coach Thunderbird. "Coach, Meowlody has a killer case of zombie fleas, and she needs my help," she said.

Coach Thunderbird nodded and motioned Toralei to the gym doors but called after her, "Hurry back, Stripe! Pitchforks wait for no monster!"

Frankie ran to Draculaura and Clawdeen.

Draculaura groaned as she transformed into her bat form to avoid the flying pitchfork Heath threw. "Exactly how bad can I be at dodge-pitchfork and still get an A?"

"You'll be fine," Clawdeen said, jumping up and snatching a pitchfork out of the air. "As long as you grunt and scream a lot, Coach Thunderbird will be happy."

"That sounds terrible," Draculaura responded, morphing back into her monster form in a puff of pink smoke.

Frankie cleared their throat, ignoring the pitchfork that sailed close to their ear and brushed their hair. "Um, Toralei is going to make an EekTok update."

"Well this game just took a right turn into Grossville and landed on Vile Avenue," Clawdeen said, launching a pitchfork back at the opposing team with more force than necessary.

Another pitchfork sailed at Frankie, and they grabbed it by the handle.

"Launch it back, Stein!" Coach Thunderbird shouted, her whistle blowing as she spoke.

A small spark shot out from Frankie's hand as they launched the pitchfork directly toward Deuce on the other team. The now-electrified pitchfork caught Deuce's gray ski cap with its tines and knocked it off his head. His snakes slithered upward and stuck their tongues out at Frankie.

"Sssuper throw," Pride said, its orange eyes on Frankie.

"That tickled, Frankie," Deuce laughed, an electric spark traveling down from his ear to the back of his neck.

"Sorry, Deuce," Frankie called, waving their hands in the air.

"Stein! There's no apologizing in dodge pitchfork," Coach Thunderbird yelled, her wings on her hips.

Once the game was over, Draculaura, Clawdeen, and Frankie gathered in the corner of the gym.

"Do you have your iCoffin?" Clawdeen asked Draculaura. "Has Toralei made her update?"

Draculaura pulled out her phone and scrolled through EekTok. "It doesn't look like she's posted anything new."

"Well, thank goodness. The less she posts about Frankie having a brain part from the sachamama, the better."

"AAAHHH!" Spectra screeched as she popped up from the floor. "Wait, what did you say?"

Frankie's eyes grew wide, and sparks shot out from their fingers.

"Nothing!" Clawdeen said. "I was just . . . uh, reviewing Draculaura and Frankie's performance in dodge pitchfork with them. You know, there's always room for improvement."

Spectra raised an eyebrow. "Really? I could've sworn I heard something about a sachamama."

Draculaura shook her head enthusiastically, the pink bow in her hair almost falling off. "Oh no, Frankie was just telling us about their mom. Their, uh, mama."

Spectra shrugged and sailed through the gym. She snuck up behind Heath and screamed. He immediately launched a pitchfork at Spectra that sailed right through her.

Scuffing their foot on the gym floor, Frankie said, "So I think the best idea right now is to go to the library, right?"

Draculaura looked at Frankie and smiled. "Well, yeah, the library is always a good idea. But why specifically do we need to go there?"

Frankie bit their lip. They lowered their voice to a whisper. "I had a vision about Dr. Hemlock. She was a student at Monster High."

"She was what?!?" Clawdeen cried, her voice echoing.

Every eye, tentacle, and wing in the gym turned toward the trio. Spectra put her hands on her hips and narrowed her eyes.

Clawdeen dismissed them with a wave of her hand. "Don't mind me. Just getting the gossip from our favorite terrornovela. You know, all drama, all the time."

Draculaura grabbed Clawdeen and Frankie by the arms. "Let's get out of here before anyone says something they shouldn't. Zip your lips."

"My lips don't zip," Frankie said. "But at least Manny in the library knows everything and might have information for us."

Draculaura grunted as they walked down the hall toward the library. "He doesn't know everything."

Clawdeen shrugged. "But he might have information about you-know-who being a student at you-know-where."

When they got to the library, Draculaura marched right up to the circulation desk where Manny was sorting through returned books. She put her hands on her hips and stared up at him.

"We need information," she said.

Manny nodded slowly, intimidated by Draculaura even though he stood three feet taller than her and could probably toss her up to the ceiling with his pinky finger. "Well, uh, we have plenty of that, don't ya know."

"How would we find out about students who used to be at Monster High?" Clawdeen asked.

Manny looked at her and his shoulders relaxed. "Oh, that's easy. I think we have every single Monster High fearbook going back forever. Are you looking for a particular student or a particular year?"

Draculaura and Clawdeen glanced expectantly at Frankie. They twisted their finger around the blue streak in their hair. A small electric spark shot from their finger and curled the streak into tight frizz.

Clawdeen smiled at Frankie and turned back to Manny. "We heard a rumor that Dr. Valeria Hemlock was a student at Monster High. You know, that scientist everyone's been talking about?"

Manny's eyes grew wide. "Really? That's amazing!"

Frankie looked at Manny as he stepped out from behind the circulation desk. "You don't think that's a bad thing?"

Manny shrugged his wide shoulders. "Well, gosh, you know she was a supersmart scientist. That means she's learned a lot of what she knew right here. I don't mean to brag or anything, but I'd say that's pretty great for Monster High."

"You should have an EekTok account," Frankie blurted out.

Clawdeen laughed and patted Frankie on the back. "Yeah, it might be good to drown out some other noise on there."

"Oh, no thank you. Now if you'll follow me, please, I can show you where we keep all of the fearbooks," Manny said, leading the trio through the library, between rows of books and to a corner with a short bookshelf. Each book on the shelf had a year printed on the spine.

Manny pulled a fearbook off the shelf. A large *M* resting on top of an *H* was printed on the cover in pink and blue. "Excuse me, but do we know what years Dr. Hemlock—"

"Shhh!" Draculaura said. "Let's keep it quiet about . . . that person."

"You-know-who!" Frankie corrected.

Clawdeen pulled five fearbooks off the shelf and handed them to Draculaura. Then she grabbed five for Frankie and five more for herself. They settled in at a table in the library while Manny gripped twenty fearbooks in his hands and sat down with them.

"Is it okay if I help?" he asked sheepishly, his chair creaking under him as he shifted his weight. "I like research."

"Of course!" Frankie said. "Statistically, the more participants we have, the more likely we are to complete this project. Whoa, thanks, zombie mathematician!"

The large ghoulfather clock in the library ticked off minutes as Draculaura, Clawdeen, Frankie, and Manny flipped through fearbook pages, searching for Dr. Hemlock. They became so engrossed in reading that when Skullette suddenly blared an announcement, they all jumped.

"MONSTERS! PLEASE AVOID THE SOUTH WING OF THE SCHOOL DUE TO THE SHAKING WALLS UNLESS YOU WANT TO BE CRUSHED BY FALLING STONES AND BURIED IN THE SCHOOL CEMETERY. OH WAIT . . . SCRATCH THAT. JUST AVOID THE SOUTH WING BECAUSE THE SHAKING IS GIVING STUDENTS MOTION SICKNESS."

Frankie and their friends searched through every single fearbook, pouring over pictures of the very first fearleading squad, the opening of the Coffin Bean, all the previous talent shows, and even an ill-fated dodge pitchfork tournament.

But no Dr. Hemlock.

"Are you sure you saw what you think you did?" Draculaura asked Frankie.

Frankie shrugged and bit their lip. "Dr. Hemlock was sitting right here in the library when I had the flashback. She was studying, but everything was noisy. So, she went and wandered around Monster High to find a quieter place to study. But maybe I was wrong?"

Clawdeen shook her head. "No, if that's what you say you saw, we believe you. She's got to be in here somewhere."

Manny sucked in a breath and slid an open fear-book from forty years ago to the center of the table. "Excuse me but I think I found her."

Draculaura, Clawdeen, and Frankie leaned in and stared at the page in the yearbook. There was a large picture of a girl in a white lab coat with long black hair and pale skin. She was holding a beaker filled with green liquid in one hand and a gold medal in the other hand. Underneath the photo, the caption read *Valeria Hemlock, winner of the Monster High Scary Science Competition.*

Frankie examined Dr. Hemlock's face. Instead of looking excited about winning a medal, her lips were pressed in a tight line. There were dark circles under her eyes, and her lab coat was slightly wrinkled.

"She looks very serious, doesn't she?" Draculaura commented.

Frankie didn't say anything, but they couldn't help thinking it wasn't seriousness that made Dr. Hemlock look that way. When Frankie closed their eyes, they could picture blackness with a faint green light growing in a corner. But they couldn't make out what it was or what it meant.

Clawdeen flipped through the pages of the fearbook. "Maybe there's something else in here about her."

"Sorry, but wait a second," Manny said, as Clawdeen paused on a page. "Look at that. I heard about that kid."

Frankie read the fearbook page Manny was

pointing at. At the top in large letters, it said *Monster High Remembers Eric Arachnidson.*

"Who is that?" Draculaura asked. "And what happened to him?"

Frankie looked at the picture of a boy in the center of the page. His skin was gray and he had a red symbol on his forehead, like what Frankie had seen on black widow spiders. Two white fangs poked out from his lips, which were stretched in a wide smile. His short black hair stuck up in all directions from his head.

Underneath the picture, the caption said, *Student Eric Arachnidson went missing during his second year as a student at Monster High. We appreciate the efforts of students who searched the campus for him and will always remember his presence at our school.*

Frankie brushed their hand over the page. Around the picture, various students had written their own tributes to Eric.

We'll never forget how fangtastic you were!

*Thanks for always helping me
in boo-ology class!*

*Monster High will
remember you forever!*

"He disappeared," Frankie said. "Somewhere here at school, and they never found him."

Clawdeen gave a nervous chuckle. "Gee, I always thought Skullette's announcements about students facing certain doom if they wandered into the wrong part of school were just exaggerations. Can it really happen? Because I'm gonna have to take those *way* more seriously from now on."

Draculaura shrugged. "I guess so."

Manny cleared his throat. "Um, look at this," he said.

With a large finger, Manny pointed to a picture at the bottom of the fearbook page. Eric Arachnidson stood in the middle of the gym, his arms filled with small skulls. He was surrounded by a few other students. One student held up a sign that read *Monster*

High Skull Juggling Champion. But in the corner of the gym, barely looking at the camera, was a girl whose lips were pressed into a scowl, and her black eyes were narrowed.

It was Valeria Hemlock.

Someone had drawn a circle around Valeria's face and written one word next to it in messy letters.

Guilty?

Everyone stared at the picture and the writing in silence.

Until Manny finally spoke up and said what everyone was thinking but too afraid to say.

"Sorry, but . . . you don't think she had something to do with Eric's disappearance, do you?"

CHAPTER 12

Frankie looked from Manny to Draculaura and Clawdeen. The butterflies in their stomach swirled as Frankie twisted their hands in their lap. They opened their mouth to speak, but their tongue didn't work. The synapses in their brain weren't firing, keeping Frankie still and staring out the window. Through the glass, Frankie could see a group of students at the edge of the casketball court, all looking at their phones.

Only one word slid across the hills and valleys of their brain.

Guilty.

Draculaura waved her hand dismissively. "Oh, I'm sure Dr. Hemlock had nothing to do with that. A monster would never hurt another monster."

Clawdeen bit her lip and tapped her finger on the table. "But . . . I hate to say this, how do we know for sure? We weren't there. And we've already decided we don't know enough about sachamamas to say whether they'd hurt anyone, monster or human."

Frankie looked at Clawdeen, still unable to say anything. Their brain was beginning to energize again, but none of their thoughts made sense. All their brain parts kept shouting over one another. Frankie looked around the library, not wanting to see Draculaura, Clawdeen, or Manny's expressions. They'd rather stare at books flying randomly off shelves, at the window in the far corner of the library shaking gently as the stones around it quivered, or at Twyla Boogeyman sitting behind a tall stack of books reading. Anything but the doubtful looks on their friends' faces.

"Frankie?" Draculaura whispered as she reached across the table and slid her hand over her friend's. "Are you OK?"

Frankie wanted to say yes. Frankie wanted to assure their friends that everything was fine. That they had absolutely no problem having a brain part from someone who was not only a monster surrounded by terrible rumors but also a scientist who might have done experiments on humans, and now someone who may have made a Monster High student disappear.

But that was a lot to be OK with.

An electric spark shot from Frankie's ear to the fearbook, slamming it shut with a bang.

"This is confusing," Frankie finally said, their voice barely a whisper.

Draculaura squeezed Frankie's hand. "I know it is. But we're going to figure this out."

"There's so much to figure out," Frankie said, their lip quivering.

Manny looked at Frankie and smiled. "Just a small suggestion, but when I have a lot of research to do, I usually make a list, so I don't get lost in all the steps I'm trying to complete."

"I do that, too," Draculaura added quickly, giving Frankie a thumbs-up.

Clawdeen pulled a blank piece of paper from a stack on the table as Manny handed her the pencil from behind his ear. "So, let's make a list. And let's go in order," she said.

Draculaura clapped her hands together and rolled her shoulders back. This was her time to shine. "First, we should figure out if Dr. Hemlock had anything to do with Eric Arachnidson disappearing," she said.

"Then maybe that will give us clues about what Dr. Hemlock was like as a scientist," Manny added. "Proving she's not guilty of Eric's disappearance might mean she's not guilty of making humans disappear, either."

Frankie turned to Manny and looked him up and down. "Do you really think she's innocent?"

Manny shrugged. "I think maybe monsters shouldn't be accused of terrible things when they might not have done them in the first place. You know, I've read about Dr. Hemlock. She was an incredible scientist. Don't you think she deserves a fair chance?"

Clawdeen smiled and nudged Frankie with her elbow. Frankie squared their shoulders and said, "Well, then I should tell you that I have a brain part from Dr. Hemlock. And she wasn't just a brilliant scientist, like you said. She was a sachamama, too. So that means I'm part sachamama, right?"

Frankie, Clawdeen, and Draculaura waited for Manny to react to the mountain of information Frankie had just dumped on him. But they didn't have to wait long.

A broad smile broke out on Manny's face. "Well, gee, that's amazing. I've only read about sachamamas in books. And now there's one standing right in front of me?"

"Part of one," Frankie corrected. "So, you're OK with all of this?"

Manny nodded. "Oh, sure. You're Frankie, multi-talented monster extraordinaire. And this list we're working through is going to prove that to everyone."

Frankie smiled at Manny, grateful to have another friend on board. There was still a lot they had to figure out, but it felt good to tell another monster the truth. They felt just a little lighter.

Clawdeen chuckled and scanned the list again. "Once we figure out if Dr. Hemlock had anything to do with Eric Arachnidson's disappearance, then all of that might help us figure out what sachamamas are really like, since they seem to be surrounded by more rumor than fact," Clawdeen said, scribbling on the paper.

Frankie took a deep breath. "And then maybe it will be OK that I have a brain part from Dr. Hemlock. Maybe people won't think that's a bad thing, right?"

Clawdeen put her hand on Frankie's back. "It's not a bad thing! And if anyone says otherwise—"

"Your nails are digging into my back," Frankie said.

Clawdeen took her hand off Frankie and ran her fingers through her curls. "Sorry."

Draculaura took the list from Clawdeen and looked it over. "Frankie, you said you saw a vision of Dr. Hemlock at Monster High as a student. Do you think you could force yourself to have another vision so that maybe we could learn more about her and this situation with Eric Arachnidson?"

Frankie pursed their lips. "That vision popped into my brain because my hand short-circuited and I replaced it with one that had garden tools on it."

"That's not a sentence you hear every day," Clawdeen smiled at Frankie.

"If only we could somehow tap into your subconscious. Then we could see more about Dr. Hemlock," Manny said, drumming his finger on the table. "Of course, only if that's OK with you."

Frankie scanned the library again. There were still books flying off shelves, but this time it was because the floor of the library was shaking, just like the window in the far corner. The stack of books Twyla Boogeyman was reading tumbled, and she scrambled to collect them.

Twyla looked at Frankie and their friends and marched over to them.

Twisting the bracelet on her wrist, Twyla said, "These books are being very loud. And so are you."

"Sorry about that, Twyla," Frankie said. "We're trying to figure out a big problem."

She always sat in the back row in all the classes that Frankie had with her, but Twyla was one of the smartest students Frankie knew at Monster High, including Draculaura and Manny. Everyone knew that certain noises bothered Twyla and that she didn't like to be touched. She was happiest in the quiet library.

Twyla rotated her bracelet around her wrist. "Big problems need big solutions. Like when I read about how an entire sanctuary was created for chupacabras after their habitat was destroyed."

"Exactly! Would you be OK joining me and my friends at our table so we could explain it to you?" Frankie asked, trying their best not to send nervous sparks out of their fingers that would startle Twyla.

Twyla eyed the stacks of books on her table, and for a moment, Frankie was afraid Twyla would say no and just go back to her reading. Instead, Twyla said, "Let's do it."

Manny hopped up, knocking his knee on the corner of the table and causing the wood to splinter. He pulled out a chair for Twyla, and she sat down. She stared at the crack in the tabletop instead of looking at anyone.

Once Frankie returned to their seat, they explained everything about their brain part from Dr.

Hemlock and the mystery behind Eric Arachnidson's disappearance.

Twyla nodded. "I read all about that. Apparently, everyone's surprised Dr. Hemlock died so young. Sachamamas usually live much longer, assuming they get enough sunlight for photosynthesis."

"Hold up," Clawdeen said. "One mystery at a time. First, we need to figure out a way to help Frankie access Dr. Hemlock's memories through their brain part."

Twyla looked at Frankie and shrugged as she popped her bracelet against her wrist. "That shouldn't be a problem. I can enter other monsters' dreams, you know. Like, see inside their minds."

"Oh!" Clawdeen exclaimed. "Could you help Frankie see information from their brain parts?"

Draculaura's eyes grew wide. "If Twyla could gain access to Frankie's subconscious and access Dr. Hemlock's memories about being at Monster High and about Eric Arachnidson, we'd be one step closer to solving this mystery."

Manny looked at Twyla. "Only if you would be OK with that, of course."

The group waited for Twyla to speak. A small smile tugged on the corner of her mouth, and she began drumming her fingers on the table, counting each one.

"An adventure. It might not be better than one of my books, but I could give it a try," Twyla said, her voice soft and barely filling the library air.

Frankie smiled. "So, how exactly do we do this? Gotta plug you into my brain somehow? Download information like on a computer?"

The smile tugging at Twyla's mouth grew wider. "That's not a boogeyman. Shadows and dreams. That's a boogeyman."

Twyla got up from her chair and moved over to Frankie. She brushed her hands on her light pink skirt and then reached her hands out toward Frankie's temples. The lights in the library flickered, the shadows growing across the walls in black streaks. When Twyla's fingertips touched Frankie's skin, their green and blue eyes turned white as they took in a sharp breath.

"Hang on!" Clawdeen suddenly said, slamming her hands down on the table.

Twyla dropped her hands to her sides and clenched her fists, staring at the ground.

"What's wrong?" Frankie asked, their eyes returning to their regular color.

Clawdeen sighed. "It's probably not the best idea to conduct what is practically a séance in the middle of the library for anyone to see, all while a particular student is roaming around looking for excuses to dig up dirt on you."

"I'm not Ghoulia. There's no dirt and there's nothing to dig up," Frankie said, their eyebrows scrunching together in confusion.

"That's not what I mean. We need to watch out for Toralei. No need to give her another reason to spread any more rumors about you," Clawdeen said.

"Toralei's rumors are about Frankie. That makes sense," Twyla said, rotating her bracelet around her wrist as she eyed a shelf of books about the Great Yeti Migration. "You all talk loudly for being in the library. I heard everything."

"Oh. Um, yeah," Clawdeen said, biting her lip and looking at Frankie.

Draculaura rolled her eyes. "I swear this school has ears everywhere," she said with a groan.

Frankie tilted their head to the side. "I thought it was made of stone and wood. Haven't seen any ears. No noses either."

Twyla looked at Frankie and made eye contact with them for the first time. "We should keep you safe," she said.

Turning away from Frankie, Twyla walked out of the library.

Manny looked at Draculaura, Clawdeen, and Frankie. "Do we . . . do we follow her?"

Frankie hopped up from their chair. "Well, she said it would be an adventure. Let's go!"

CHAPTER 13

Twyla led Frankie and their friends through the halls of Monster High as the walls shook, doors appeared out of nowhere, and staircases still moved in unexpected directions. No matter which hallway they chose, it was as if the school was trying to lead them deeper and deeper into the catacombs underneath the building.

"This school has a mind of its own!" Clawdeen groaned as the group went through a large red door and ended up on the first floor instead of the third, like they wanted.

"This school isn't human or monster," Frankie said. "It's impossible for it to have a brain."

"Brain or no brain, Monster High usually does its own thing," Draculaura said.

"Although, I've never seen it quite this bad."

Manny stepped on a stair gently, checking to see if it was going to move. When it stayed in place, he waved the rest of the group up the steps.

"You know, I read in *The Architectural History of Monster High, Volume Three*, that the school reacts when a student needs help," he said as they all walked up the stairs, their hands on the railing in case the steps decided to move suddenly.

"That's one of my favorite books," Twyla said.

"What kinds of things does the school do?" Frankie asked.

Manny nodded. "Well, it said several years ago there was a student who was trying out for the casketball team and was getting frustrated because they couldn't ever practice on the casketball court. So, Monster High turned every locker in the school into a casketball coffin. The student got in trouble with Headmistress Bloodgood for dunking in everyone's locker, but they made the team."

"Casketball coffins everywhere?" Clawdeen exclaimed as the group made their way through a door that thankfully led to the north wing of the school instead of the creepateria. "That would be clawsome!"

Manny chuckled. "There were lots of examples like that, you know. Like if a student needed a quiet place to study, they might open a door and find an abandoned mummy tomb they can work in. Or if they needed a way to make sure they always got to class on time, the stairs would suddenly be covered in goo monster slime. Stuff like that."

Draculaura thought for a moment. "But all this shaking seems a lot more severe than just casketball coffins and study rooms."

"Should we add it to our list of things to research?" Frankie asked.

"I'm sure I've read a book about that somewhere," Twyla said.

Clawdeen shook her head. "We don't have any more room on our list. We've got too much to figure out as it is!"

After dodging a swinging chandelier that tried to push everyone through an open door, Twyla ended up in front of one of the many practice rooms that students had been using to prepare for the talent show. When they all got settled in the room, Frankie could smell the faint scent of burnt paper and saw black streaks on one of the curtains. They were fairly certain Heath was the last student to use the room.

"What should we do now?" Draculaura asked, looking around the empty room. There were four claw-shaped lanterns on each wall but nothing else.

Twyla sat cross-legged in the middle of the floor and pointed in front of her. "Lay here," she said to Frankie.

Stretching out on the ground, Frankie settled with their head toward Twyla's lap.

Twyla pointed to the spaces around Frankie but didn't break her gaze from Frankie's head and said, "You all sit around them. It's best if we're in a circle."

The girls sat on either side of Frankie, and Manny sat at their feet.

Once again, Twyla gently placed her fingers on Frankie's temples. Frankie's breathing slowed as their eyes swirled with a white film. The lights in the room flickered and, one by one, turned off, plunging the room into darkness.

A glowing blue light emanated from Twyla's chest, creating shadows behind the group. The shadows stretched across the wall, crawling over each crack and stone.

"What's happening?" Clawdeen whispered, her eyes darting to the black shapes.

Draculaura shushed her and looked at Frankie. They were in a trance, breathing deeply.

"But how will we know what Frankie is seeing?" Clawdeen said, leaning over to Manny.

He didn't answer, his eyes glued on Twyla as her mouth opened and closed.

Finally, she spoke, her voice echoing softly around the room.

"I see a girl walking down a hallway. She has long black hair and pale skin. The hallway looks like Monster High. Now she's going through a door and down a dark corridor. The stairs in front of her wind down, down, down."

"That has to be Dr. Hemlock," Draculaura said.

Twyla took a deep breath, the blue light coming from her chest growing, traveling down her arms, and bouncing between her fingertips and Frankie's temples. Frankie still lay completely motionless, their eyes now closed. But when Draculaura looked at Frankie's eyelids, it was obvious that their eyes were moving back and forth, like when someone is in a deep dream.

"The girl is going down the stairs. She's searching again. Now she's in a room filled with overgrown plants. Or maybe it's just one plant. There are vines everywhere. She's sitting in a corner of the room, a notebook in her lap. She's writing away in the notebook. She looks happy to be alone in a quiet place," Twyla said, staring straight ahead at Manny but not really looking at him.

But then Twyla's eyebrows knit together. She leaned slightly forward as if she was trying to get a better look at something no one else could see. The black shadows swirled on the walls in a feverish dance. Manny hunched his shoulders, trying to make himself as small as possible.

Draculaura reached across Frankie and grabbed Clawdeen's hand.

"Wait, she's not alone. I can't . . . I can't see," Twyla mumbled. "I can't see who it is. There's someone else."

Twyla's breathing increased and a small whimper came from Frankie on the floor.

The walls of the practice room began to shake. One of the light fixtures crashed to the floor with a loud smash. Draculaura jumped, and Clawdeen yelped. Manny drew his knees to his chest, eyeing a hole in the wall that formed when the light fell.

"Just a little longer," Twyla said, her voice louder than it had ever been, as if she was calling into the darkness. "I can almost see them."

A small green vine shot out from between the stones in the wall, crept across the floor, and wrapped around Frankie's ankle.

"Look out!" Clawdeen shouted. She tried to pull the vine off Frankie's foot, but the plant just coiled around Frankie's ankle tighter.

"Frankie! Wake up!" Draculaura shouted.

"No! I can almost see!" Twyla screeched and bent forward over Frankie.

Manny tried to stomp on the vine, his thick foot shaking the floor, but the vine twisted and curled out of the way each time. Manny stumbled, and his wide shoulder bumped into Clawdeen. Clawdeen fell into Twyla, knocking her fingers off Frankie's head. The loss of contact made the light coming from her chest disappear.

Frankie's eyes flew open. "Zaps!" they exclaimed.

The vine traveled from Frankie's foot and up their calf. It began to pull and drag Frankie's body toward an opening in the wall that had grown after the light fixture fell to the floor. The stones around the hole grew teeth and looked like they were trying to devour Frankie whole.

Frankie sat up and slapped at the vine. "Should've kept my garden tool hand," they said.

"Hurry, Frankie! Do something!" Draculaura shouted.

Frankie grabbed the vine and squeezed, an electric spark shooting from their palm. The vine immediately released Frankie's ankle and turned a light gray. As it snaked back into the wall and disappeared, Manny tilted his head to the side.

"Excuse me, but did any of you hear that?" he asked, scratching his head.

"What?" Clawdeen asked, smoothing down her hair with her hands.

Manny shrugged. "It sounded like it said 'ouch.'"

"Last time I checked, plants don't talk," Clawdeen said.

Draculaura chuckled. "This is Monster High, though."

Frankie turned toward Twyla. "Did you see him like I did? Did you see who he was?" they asked, breathless.

Twyla looked at her hands in her lap and slowly shook her head. "Too much. Too much noise."

Clawdeen rushed over to Twyla and started to put her hand on her back but stopped, unsure if that would comfort Twyla. "Is it okay if I hug you? Is there anything I can do to help you feel better?"

Twyla's breathing calmed down and she gave a small nod. "Will you squeeze my hand?"

Clawdeen wrapped both hands around Twyla's.

"We did it," Twyla said to Frankie.

"Thank you, Twyla," Frankie said. "We really did it. I saw him."

"Who did you see?" Draculaura asked, hopping up and turning the lights back on in the practice room. The hole in the wall had completely closed, no evidence left that it had ever existed.

Frankie looked at Draculaura, Clawdeen, and Manny.

"It was Eric Arachnidson. He was in the catacombs of Monster High with Dr. Hemlock."

CHAPTER 14

𖣯 💀 𖣯

Frankie sat in home ick class the next day, looking from student to student after their teacher, Mx. Cucuy, announced they were each supposed to pair up for a new class project. Draculaura and Clawdeen were sitting right next to each other and immediately paired up. Frankie didn't mind, because they assumed they'd be able to find another partner. But Lagoona wouldn't make eye contact with Frankie, and Heath scooted his chair away from them right after Mx. Cucuy finished talking. Abbey Abominable and Skelita Calaveras distracted themselves with the dough on their table and wouldn't even look at Frankie. Cleo had started to walk over to Frankie, but Purrsephone pulled her back and started whispering in her ear.

Were Toralei's videos making everyone at Monster High believe Frankie was a sachamama? Had they figured out her first clue?

"Looks like it's just you and me, Frankie," Deuce said, sliding his chair over to Frankie's table. "OK with you if we work together?"

Deuce rubbed the back of his neck as one of the snakes under his ski cap tickled it with its tongue. Frankie had read that gorgons like Deuce were always mean. Once, when Deuce's mom, Medusa, had visited the school, Frankie even heard her announce that gorgons were never nice. But the more Frankie talked to Deuce, the more they disagreed with that hypothesis.

Frankie nodded and started to knead the ball of dough on the table. But as they tried to shape the pastry into a sculpture of Watzie, they couldn't stop thinking about what they'd seen in the practice room.

Dr. Hemlock had been sitting in a room with overgrown plants somewhere deep in the school, but they weren't alone. Eric Arachnidson was also with them.

Did that mean they were friends? That they worked together?

Or could it possibly suggest that Dr. Hemlock had something to do with Eric's disappearance?

All Frankie could focus on was those questions and not the pastry in front of them. The wings Frankie kept trying to shape on dough-Watzie's back began to fall apart, crumbling all over the metal table.

"Hey, Frankie?" Deuce said, leaning over to them. "If you use egg mixed with water, it'll help your dough pieces stay together better."

Pride peeked out from under Deuce's hat and hissed at Frankie. "He'sss alwaysss right."

Frankie shook their head, bringing their thoughts back to the classroom, the project in front of them, and Deuce. "Oh, thanks! Would be nice to have a famous chef up here, right?" Frankie said, pointing to their head.

"There'sss no room here," Greed, another of Deuce's snakes, said.

Deuce batted the snake away with his hand. "Everything OK? You seem like your brain is on another planet," he said.

Frankie stopped rolling a small bit of dough between their fingers. "Oh, my brain is right here. It hasn't gone anywhere, especially not to outer space."

Deuce chuckled and turned back to his pastry sculpture, rolling a long section of dough on the table under his hand. He took a knife and quickly cut small scales into the dough. And then as a final touch, he placed two small pieces of dough at one end for eyes and pinched another piece into a small triangle for a tongue.

"It's a pastry snake!" Frankie exclaimed.

Three snakes looked out from under Deuce's hat at his creation. "We look sssuperior," they said in union.

"Actually, I think this is good enough to make it into my notebook," Deuce said.

"Your notebook?" Frankie asked, trying to shape a piece of dough into a tail for Watzie.

Deuce nodded, sliding an orange book over to Frankie. "I keep a notebook of all my recipes. That makes it easier to keep track of what I've tried and to make adjustments to recipes I'm still trying to figure out."

Deuce opened the notebook to show Frankie a picture of cookies in the shape of Cerberus, with each head of the three-headed dog a different flavor. When Frankie reached out to flip the page, their hand gripped the notebook tightly, and a spark shot from their ear to the base of their neck, straightening their back.

Instead of the home ick classroom, Frankie saw the same room underneath the school that Dr. Hemlock had found to study in peace and quiet. A notebook was open on Dr. Hemlock's lap, a page covered with equations and drawings of plants. A gray finger pointed to a drawing of a spider on the page, and Frankie's gaze traveled up the arm to the face of the person pointing. It was Eric Arachnidson.

Frankie's grip released Deuce's notebook. "They were working together!" they blurted out.

Deuce raised his eyebrow at Frankie. "Huh?"

Frankie shrugged and chuckled nervously. "Oh, it's nothing. Just a little bit of motivational speaker frontal lobe."

Placing his pastry creation on a baking sheet, Deuce laughed. "That sounds fun."

Frankie looked over at Draculaura and Clawdeen at another table in class. Frankie started to run over to their friends to tell them what they had seen, but suddenly the classroom was filled with a chiming sound as everyone's iCoffins buzzed.

The butterflies in Frankie's stomach immediately swirled, sending nervous sparks throughout Frankie's body.

Deuce pulled out his phone. "Looks like Toralei has another update. Have you figured out who she's talking about yet?"

Frankie bit their lip. "Metaphors and riddles can sometimes be difficult to decipher," they said.

Deuce hit play on the video, and Frankie looked over his shoulder.

"Hey again, Monster High," Toralei said, winking at the camera. "I've got another update for you about the sachamama. I bet you're electrified with excitement trying to figure it out. Sachamamas wait for days, sitting still to lure their prey. Laying over hill, rock, and dune . . . but our sachamama has barely seen one moon."

Frankie drummed their fingers on the table. Not concentrating, they sent a spark out from their index finger that hit a ball of dough and cooked it immediately.

"Zaps!" they said. Frankie gave a cautious look at Deuce. He was rewatching Toralei's video, his eyes narrowed at his iCoffin screen. "So do you have any idea who the sachamama is?"

Deuce shook his head. "No. But I'd sure like to meet them. My moms know all the snakes in the monster world, but they've never met a sachamama. That would be the coolest."

Frankie thought for a moment. "But aren't there a lot of bad rumors about sachamamas? Aren't they supposed to be terrible monsters?"

Shrugging, Deuce began making another snake out of dough. "People started a lot of horrible rumors about my mom, Medusa. Like how she'd turn anyone she didn't like into stone."

"Didn't she actually do that to the other parents in the PTA meeting when they voted against her fear-raising idea?" Frankie asked. "That's what Draculaura told me."

Deuce waved his hand dismissively. "Well, yeah. That did actually happen. But people have said a lot of other things about her that aren't really true. You can't believe everything you hear."

Frankie thought about Toralei's last EekTok video, where she had given the clue about the sachamama being a student and not a teacher. Mostly they thought about all the comments people had written under it. Frankie had scrolled through all of them until they couldn't read any more stories about how someone's ghoulmother's cousin knew a sachamama who had eaten the banshee mail carrier. They wished everyone thought the way Deuce did.

"Thanks, Deuce," Frankie said as they headed over to Draculaura and Clawdeen.

Clawdeen was trying to make a casketball hoop out of dough. Draculaura was crafting her pet,

Count Fabulous, in pastry form, but she couldn't decide whether to show him as a winged cat or as a bat.

"Breaking news," Frankie said, their arms crossed over their chest so tightly their shoulders nearly popped out of their sockets.

Draculaura groaned. "We already saw Toralei's latest EekTok. Everybody did. Not really sure what she's trying to say in it. Except that 'electrifying' part was a little obvious."

Clawdeen glanced around the room and whispered. "I think she's talking about how young Frankie is. One moon?"

Draculaura bit her lip, confused. Clawdeen explained further, "One month! If there's one thing werewolves know, it's the moon cycle. And one moon cycle is about thirty days."

"That's about how old I am," Frankie said, making sure no one else in the class was listening to their conversation. "But that's not my breaking news. I have information about you-know-who being a you-know-what you-know-where."

Draculaura examined Frankie's face. "I know we're trying to keep things secret, but you're going to have to be more specific than that."

Frankie leaned in and whispered, "Deuce's notebook gave me another vision about Dr. Hemlock."

"Oh!" Draculaura exclaimed loudly.

Abbey and Skelita looked up from their projects and raised their eyebrows. Mx. Cucuy narrowed their red eyes at Draculaura, who slapped her hand over her mouth.

Luckily, a piercing scream filled the air, indicating the end of class. Draculaura, Clawdeen, and Frankie hurried out of the room.

"So, what was the vision?" Draculaura asked after looking around and making sure Toralei was nowhere in sight.

"She was working with Eric Arachnidson on something. Her notebook was filled with equations and drawings of plants. Eric was there and he was pointing to a drawing of a spider," Frankie explained.

Draculaura and Clawdeen took in all the information.

"What should we do next?" Clawdeen asked.

Frankie stopped in their tracks and clenched their fists, concentrating. "If we can find Dr. Hemlock's notebooks, maybe we can figure out what she was working on with Eric. And that would help us figure out what happened to Eric, hopefully proving Dr. Hemlock's innocence. And then we'd know more about her work as a scientist and her life as a sachamama."

"The notebooks are the key," Draculaura said. "We find those, all the items on our list start getting checked off one after the other. Like dominoes falling over."

"No, now's not the time to play games. We have too much to do," Frankie said.

Clawdeen patted Frankie on the back and laughed as the trio headed toward the library.

As they walked away, they were too occupied by their conversation to notice that a small green vine had shot out of the wall and slithered along the floor, following them.

CHAPTER 15

rankie, Draculaura, and Clawdeen found Manny and Twyla in the library, as expected. Except this time, Twyla was sitting at the table closest to the circulation desk, where Manny was working, two stacks of books neatly piled up in front of her.

When Manny saw the trio enter the library, he took a big breath and squared his wide shoulders. "Oh gee, are we going on another adventure?" he asked, his voice shaking just a bit.

Clawdeen smirked and winked at Manny. "How familiar are you with the catacombs underneath the school? Got any info for us in that big brain of yours?"

Manny scratched his head. "Well, I've read every volume of *The Architectural History of Monster High*, but no one knows when this school was built. So, I'm sure sorry, but I can't tell you how old they are. And there aren't any maps of the catacombs, since it seems like their shape is always changing."

"Is that your way of saying you don't know much about them?" Draculaura asked, her arms crossed.

Manny shrugged. "I guess."

Frankie sat down next to Twyla, who was busy reading a book. Without stopping, she reached for the top book in the stack in front of her and slid it across to Frankie.

Frankie looked at the title of the book, *Thirteen Creepy Crawly Tales of Poison Plant Horror,* by V. H. Sachs.

"We're looking for you-know-who's notebooks. That particular scientist that everyone is talking about. That one whose last name is the same as one of the most poisonous plants in the world," Frankie said, drumming their fingers on the cover of the book Twyla gave them.

"Got it," Manny said, winking.

"The last place I saw the notebooks was in a vision in the catacombs under the school. So, we're arranging a search party for them," Frankie continued.

No one said anything for a moment.

Draculaura looked at Clawdeen and whispered, "We are?"

Twyla got up from her seat at the table without a word, gathered her books, and slipped them one by one into the return slot at the circulation desk.

"Another adventure. Let's go to the catacombs," she said quietly, walking out of the library.

Clawdeen clapped. "Off into the dark underground of Monster High. Let's go!"

Draculaura nodded with a smile. "Definitely."

The rest of them filed out of the library and followed Twyla.

Out of the corner of their eye, Frankie saw a flash of orange sneaking around a corner and running under some stairs. Frankie jogged and caught up with Draculaura.

"I think Toralei might be following us," they said.

"Oh bats," Draculaura said, glancing over her shoulder.

Two flashes of gray passed behind the group, hiding behind garbage goblins, next to lockers, and in shadows.

"Looks like Meowlody and Purrsephone are with her, too," Clawdeen added. She flexed her hand, and her nails grew out from her fingers.

Draculaura put her hand on Clawdeen's arm. "Wait. Look," she said, pointing to Twyla.

Next to Manny, Twyla was wiggling her fingers at her sides. The shadows stretching under the lights lining the hallway pulled away from the wall, slithered across the floor, and meandered behind Draculaura, Frankie, and Clawdeen. Then they shot up in the air, making a barrier between the group headed to the catacombs and Toralei's crew.

"Where'd they go?" Purrsephone growled.

Frankie heard a crash and a yelp as a garbage goblin tumbled across the floor.

"I can't see anything!" Meowlody whined.

As the group turned down a hallway, Twyla's shadows followed them and covered their tracks. Frankie heard Toralei exclaim, "Ugh! Fine. I guess I'll just have to update EekTok instead!"

Frankie sighed. "Thanks, Twyla," they whispered.

"No problem. I've read lots of examples of how to avoid unwanted followers. Like how to get a werebadger off your tracks," Twyla said. She led Frankie, Draculaura, Clawdeen, and Manny through the hallways of the school, down staircases, and around corners. This time, nothing in Monster High changed. The stairs stayed in their place, and no mysterious doors popped up along the walls.

Twyla finally stopped in front of a large wooden door. Writing appeared across the front, reading, FINALLY! YOU'RE HERE!

"I think it actually wants us to go down to the catacombs," Draculaura said. "Maybe the school has been trying to get us to come here this whole time, with all the doors popping up and stairs moving."

"That doesn't make me feel any better about this," Clawdeen groaned. "What if it's just excited that five students are about to walk into the dark so it can eat them?"

Manny bit his lip. "I'm sorry, but there's a slight chance your imagination is running away with you."

Frankie looked Clawdeen up and down. "But she's not running anywhere. She's right here."

Twyla opened the door, the hinges creaking and echoing in the empty hallway. The corridor beyond the door was completely black, the lights along the walls extinguished.

"Darkness," Twyla said, tapping her fingers at her sides.

"Any chance you can manipulate those shadows like you did with Toralei and her crew?" Clawdeen asked, squinting her eyes and peering through the door.

Twyla shrugged and looked at the floor. "There's no light. No light means no shadows. There's nothing to manipulate."

Frankie stepped next to Twyla. "That's OK. Hello, bionic eyes!"

Blinking once, Frankie's eyes glowed like flashlights, illuminating the way down the corridor.

"Let's go!" Frankie said, stepping through the door.

The rest followed Frankie as Manny brought up the rear, closing the door behind them to cover their tracks. Even in the darkness behind Frankie's glowing eyes, Manny could see that the door disappeared into the wall once he closed it.

"Well, I sure hope that won't be a problem later," he muttered under his breath, his hands shaking.

He tripped over a stone on the floor and bumped into Draculaura's back.

"All right," Draculaura said, rubbing her shoulder while Manny apologized profusely, "everybody be on the lookout for Dr. Hemlock's studying spot. That's where we'll find the notebooks."

Clawdeen took a deep breath. "Imagine you're Dr. Hemlock. Where would you go down here to study?"

Twyla shrugged and twisted the bracelet on her wrist. "Imagining we're Dr. Hemlock might be easier for some people than for others here."

Frankie laughed, tapping their temple with their finger. "You're not wrong."

They dragged their hand along the wall as their lights lit the path farther into the catacombs. Perhaps just the right stone, just the right touch, would trigger a memory.

The corridor eventually opened into a large room lit with small torches. Frankie blinked, and their blue and green eyes stopped glowing. The flames from the torches flickered along the walls, shadows bouncing over the stones. They looked like dark, dancing figures crawling through every inch of the catacombs.

"Twyla, could you not play with those?" Clawdeen asked. "It's frightening enough down here anyways."

Twyla held out her hands. "I'm not doing anything."

The walls of the catacombs shook, creating a deep rumble that Frankie could feel in their stomach. Specks of dirt cascaded from the ceiling, filling the air with fine dust.

"Ugh, my hair," Draculaura huffed, flipping a bright pink strand over her shoulder.

Clawdeen passed her a hair tie. "There's a bunch of pathways down here. How do we know which one to take?"

Manny squinted and looked at each tall, arching entryway to seven different paths that led from the room they were in. "Should we split up?"

Twyla coughed. "I've read seventy-six horror novels and watched eighty-three scary movies. It never ends well when people do that. Certain doom."

Frankie shook their head. "OK, so voting no for splitting up."

"I think we should just start on the left and go down each pathway until we find something. Is there anything in particular we should be looking for, Frankie?" Draculaura said, tying her hair up into a high ponytail.

Frankie bit their lip and thought for a moment. "We need to look for a room that's filled with plants. That's what was in my vision of Dr. Hemlock. Maybe that's where the notebooks are?"

"Any of these pathways look like a bunch of plants are waiting for us at the end?" Clawdeen said, waving her hand and squinting down a corridor to her left.

At just that moment, a small leaf sprouted from between the stones on the floor right in front of Twyla's shoe.

"There isn't enough light in the catacombs for photosynthesis," she said.

Frankie peered down at the leaf stretching out of the floor. Looking past it, they spotted another leaf three feet away, farther down the passageway.

"You're right. There's not enough light for photosynthesis, and germination typically doesn't occur at this rapid pace," Frankie said.

"Do I just pretend to know what you both are talking about or what?" Clawdeen said, tapping her foot on the floor.

Frankie pointed down the passageway where a third leaf sprouted out of the floor.

"It's showing us the way," they said.

CHAPTER 16

⁂

The ceiling above the catacombs shook again, sending a fresh layer of dirt down on Frankie and their friends.

"OK, let's follow the plants," Draculaura said, grabbing Clawdeen's hand. "Better than staying here and getting buried."

Frankie blinked and lit up their eyes again in the dim passageway so they could see the small leaves popping up one by one along the path. The group passed a few forks in the path, but the leaves always shot out of the ground, letting them know which option to take.

"Not to be negative, but since this is Monster High and you never know what to expect, how sure are we that these aren't the leaves from some monster-eating plant leading us to get devoured?" Clawdeen asked with a nervous chuckle.

"We don't," Frankie said matter-of-factly.

"Oh gee, that doesn't make me feel any better," Manny mumbled under his breath.

The group kept walking. They followed the plants around corners, past locked doors, down more stairs, and through even darker passageways.

"I'm not certain we're still under Monster High anymore," Draculaura whispered.

Twyla shrugged. "Space is a fluid concept. We're beneath the creepateria."

Frankie kept their eyes focused ahead to light the way, but asked, "How do you know?"

Twyla pointed a finger toward the ceiling where melted chocolate eyescream was seeping through the cracks. The three-headed chef that made all the meals for Monster High recently closed the creepateria because the tables shook too much. The students couldn't eat without throwing food everywhere. Now the leftover eyescream was melting through the floor.

"Wish we knew how far all these corridors went," Clawdeen said, straining her eyes to see farther into the catacombs.

"Easy. I can help with this," Draculaura said, transforming into a bat in a puff of pink smoke. "My bat sonar shows the two passages to the left are dead ends. Let's go to the right."

The group continued through the catacombs as Draculaura flew above them. But suddenly, Frankie stopped in their tracks, and Twyla and Clawdeen bumped into their back.

"Zaps," Frankie said. "This door doesn't look like any of the other doors we've passed."

The wooden door in front of them wasn't blocked by stones or covered in vines like some of the others they had seen as the group meandered underneath the school.

This one was covered in spiderwebs.

"Oh, no thank you," Clawdeen said. "I don't do spiders."

Frankie ran their finger along the door frame, catching some of the webs on their index finger.

Three leaves popped up at their feet right in front of the door.

"I think this is the one," Frankie said. They put their hand on the doorknob and twisted, but nothing happened. The door was sealed shut.

"Manny," Draculaura said, transforming back from her bat form. "Time to put those mile-wide shoulders to use."

Manny sheepishly rubbed the back of his neck.

"His shoulders are five thousand two hundred and seventy-six feet short of a mile," Frankie said.

Chuckling, Manny said, "True. But I think I can still open this door. I'll just make sure not to bring down the entire catacombs in the process. I'd feel really bad about that."

"Yes," Clawdeen said. "That's a fantastic goal."

Manny walked over to the cobweb-covered door and gave it a nudge with his shoulder.

Nothing happened.

Leaning in, Manny hit the door with his body a little harder. Still nothing happened.

"Manny, I'm pretty sure you could rip this door off its hinges, if you really wanted to," Draculaura said. "Show us what you've got and open it."

Manny shrugged. "Maybe you all should stand back?"

Twyla, Frankie, Draculaura, and Clawdeen took three steps back as Manny sucked in a deep breath and clenched his fists. Bending his knees, he launched himself off his front foot and threw his whole body at the door. The wood cracked and splintered, slamming open and launching Manny into the room.

The moment the door opened, a thick vine shot over Manny and slammed into the ceiling above Frankie's head. It pushed against the rocks, squirming its way between two stones, causing the walls to shake and bits of dirt and rock to fall to the ground.

"That doesn't seem good," Clawdeen said, brushing her hand on her shoulder to clean it off.

Manny stood up and straightened his shirt under his red sweater vest. "Frankie, I think we're gonna need your eyes in here."

Frankie stepped over another vine creeping out from the room and joined Manny. Their eyes lit up the dark room, revealing a tangle of leaves and vines over every wall and covering the ceiling.

Frankie took in a sharp breath as their back stiffened and their hands clenched at their sides. An electric spark shot from their ear and trailed along the top of their head.

Frankie was still in the room, but it looked different. The mess of vines covering all the walls was gone. Looking to the left, they saw Eric Arachnidson standing next to them. Frankie glanced at their hands, and their skin was covered with green veins.

Frankie was once again seeing Dr. Hemlock's memories.

"This is the perfect place for our experiments," a muffled voice said. It was coming from Frankie's throat, but it didn't sound anything like their voice.

The room shifted again, the walls rippling and settling in a new scene in front of Frankie's eyes. This time, Frankie saw themself seated on the floor, a notebook open in front of them. They handed a vial of bright green liquid to Eric.

Eric took the vial with a shaking hand. "Are you sure it's OK?" he asked. Frankie could barely hear his voice.

Frankie nodded, their fingers drumming on their knee as they watched Eric with anticipation. Their pencil hovered over their notebook, and they leaned forward as Eric placed the vial at his mouth and tilted his head back. The green liquid flowed down his throat.

He stared at Frankie for a moment—and then his eyes grew wide. He clutched his stomach and doubled over, the vial dropping from his hand and shattering on the floor.

Eric's chest heaved as his skin went from light gray to light green. The red symbol on his forehead vanished as a leaf shot through his skin and began to cover his face. Thin vines curled out of his ears. He opened his mouth to scream but coughed as leaves sprouted out of his mouth.

His muffled voice croaked, "What did you do?"

And then Eric was gone.

"Frankie!"

Snapping out of their vision, Frankie looked around the room. The vines on the wall were growing, curling across the floor, and reaching for Frankie and their friends.

Clawdeen bared her claws as a vine snaked toward her ankle. Twyla wiggled her fingers, wrapping a shadow around herself as a vine approached her. Now invisible to the approaching plant, the vine continued on its way out the door.

Another thick vine crumbled the stone wall as it shot directly toward Manny's face. Draculaura shoved with all her strength, pushing him out of the way. He fell to the ground with a thunderous huff.

"I think you enjoyed that too much," Manny said, smiling.

Draculaura shrugged. "Maybe."

A thick, dark green vine snaked up Frankie's leg and wrapped tightly around their waist. It flexed and pulled Frankie closer to the wall. Frankie looked at the leaves on the vine and gasped.

Clawdeen grabbed Frankie's hand as the vine continued to pull Frankie closer and closer to the wall where a large, blood red flower sprouted from between two stones. Its petals pulsed open and closed, as if they were chewing.

"Help me!" Clawdeen called to the others as she held tight to Frankie's arm.

Draculaura wrapped her arms around Clawdeen's waist while Manny grabbed Draculaura's hand.

Frankie's feet slid across the floor as the vine pulled them closer to the flower's chomping mouth. Squinting, Frankie peered at the center of the flower. A sharp gasp erupted from Frankie's throat, and they gripped the vine at their waist. An electric spark shot from each finger, and the vine loosened. Its green shade briefly turned light gray, and Frankie swore they heard something cry from the center of the flower.

Clawdeen gave a hard yank on Frankie's arm, and they stumbled backward. Manny scampered forward and pulled Frankie away from the vine and out of the room. Twyla, Draculaura, and Clawdeen stumbled over each other and fell out into the passageway.

Manny tried to close the door behind them, but a thick vine shot out through the opening and blocked him.

"We have to get out of here!" Draculaura shouted.

She grabbed Frankie's hand and began to pull them down the hallway, but Frankie stood firm.

"No, wait," Frankie said. "I know what that plant is."

"What are you talking about?" Clawdeen asked.

A small vine snaked out of the door and slid up Frankie's ankle. Instead of wrapping around it tightly, it rubbed against Frankie's skin.

Frankie looked down and smiled. "It's Eric."

CHAPTER 17

✢3 💀 8✢

F rankie crouched down and reached out to the vine. It curled around their finger lightly, its leaves brushing their skin.

"How is *that* Eric?" Draculaura said, narrowing her eyes at the vine.

Frankie took a deep breath. "He drank some kind of concoction that Dr. Hemlock made, and it turned him into this. I saw it. And if you look in the center of the flower, you'll see the same black widow symbol that was on Eric's head.

The thick vine above Clawdeen pushed against the ceiling, sending more dirt down on the group. She spun and jumped back onto the ground.

"I'd rather not get that close to see it," Manny said, backing away from the doorway.

Draculaura coughed and waved her hand in front of her face. "I think this is what's been causing all the shaking at Monster High. This vine has been pushing against the walls and breaking through the stones."

The vine wrapped around Frankie's finger pulled away and the leaves bent, as if nodding at Draculaura's statement.

"So now what?" Manny asked. "If that vine is Eric, how do we change him back?"

Frankie peeked into the room again. The bright red petals of the flower on the wall sagged, as if sad and tired.

Looking down again at the vine at their feet, Frankie reached out their finger and gave the vine a light shock. The color of the vine changed to light gray, but after the effect of the shock wore off, it returned to its dark green color.

"It's not enough," Frankie said, stepping back into the room. They wiggled their fingers and examined the plant covering every inch of the walls.

"What's not enough?" Clawdeen asked, peeking from behind Manny.

Frankie held up their hands. "Electric shock temporarily changes the plant back to something more Eric-like, but it doesn't last. We need to figure out something more powerful."

The vines in the room pushed and bent against the wall, sending small rocks cascading from the ceiling.

"You need to get out of there," Draculaura said, morphing into a bat in a puff of pink smoke. She grabbed the collar of Frankie's jacket with her feet and tried to pull them out of the room.

A tangle of vines in the corner spread apart and revealed a pile of cobwebs. Frankie brushed Draculaura off and took a cautious step closer to the cobwebs. They were covering something up.

"Wait," Frankie said as Draculaura changed back into her monster form. "The vine is showing me something."

Frankie spread the cobwebs apart with their fingers as the bright red flower turned and watched over their shoulder.

A pile of notebooks lay on the floor. Frankie read the writing on the first one's cover.

V. Hemlock

"These are Dr. Hemlock's notebooks!" Frankie shouted, a zap shooting from their fingers to the worn cover of the notebook at the top of the pile.

Twyla stepped back into the room and walked over to Frankie. "The solution is probably in here. The answers are always in books," she said, picking up a notebook and flipping through the pages.

Frankie grabbed another notebook and sat down on the floor. A vine curled under them, forming itself into a chair. Twyla did the same as a vine rose to prop up her back.

"I've definitely never been in a reading room like this," Manny said as he and Draculaura took cautious steps into the room. He grabbed a notebook and passed it to Draculaura before taking one for himself.

Vines curled along the floor, forming a chair for each of them.

Clawdeen blew her hair off her forehead with a sigh. "Group study date, I guess," she said. Frankie passed her a notebook as a vine curled on the floor, making a small stool.

Shaking her head, Clawdeen chuckled nervously. "Yeah, no. I'm OK with just sitting on the floor."

The sound of flipping pages filled the room as the flower on the wall watched Frankie and their friends reading through Dr. Hemlock's old notebooks.

"Excuse me, but what exactly are we looking for?" Manny asked, narrowing his eyes at a page. "I need to have a research goal."

Frankie bit their lip as their eyes scanned a page. "We need to figure out what Dr. Hemlock did to Eric. Then maybe we can figure out how to undo it."

A small chuckle echoed in the room. "If only there was someone who was uniquely qualified to interpret these equations and experiment notes," Twyla said.

Frankie looked at Twyla with a raised eyebrow. "What do you mean?"

Twyla shrugged, not looking up from the notebook in her lap. "You're the only one who can solve this, Frankie. You're the only one who can access everything Dr. Hemlock knew about plants."

Frankie sighed. "No pressure."

Minutes passed as the group flipped through Dr. Hemlock's notebooks. The walls rumbled as vines twisted across the stone. A broad leaf nudged another notebook toward Frankie, and they grabbed it. The moment their fingers touched the cover, their eyes turned white and their back stiffened.

Frankie could hear Dr. Hemlock groaning. "We've already tried three times and it didn't work," she said, her voice barely a whisper.

"But what am I gonna do?" Eric asked. "My silk is running out. What's a spider monster if he can't even make webs?"

Frankie felt Dr. Hemlock bend over her notebook. "I've already combined your monster arachnid DNA with silkworm DNA, bamboo DNA, and lotus flower DNA. None of it worked."

Eric scuffed his feet on the floor, his eyebrows raising and scrunching up the black widow symbol on his forehead. "Maybe we should stop looking at plants and animals from the human world and focus on monster DNA instead?"

The room started to fade before Frankie's eyes right as Dr. Hemlock said, "I have an idea."

Frankie's neck jerked forward, and they looked around at their friends. "You were right, Twyla. I'm the only one who can solve this."

Standing up, Frankie gripped the notebook in their hand. "These are full of Dr. Hemlock's old experiments from when she was a student here at Monster High. She was trying to help Eric because he was running out of spider silk."

"Like he was ill?" Twyla asked.

Frankie nodded. "Sounds like the type of sickness an arachnid monster would get. Dr. Hemlock tried combining his DNA with the DNA of other plants and animals in the human world, but it didn't work."

Draculaura waved her hand at the vines covering the walls. "Well, something must have finally worked. Sort of," she said.

"What sort of DNA could Dr. Hemlock have combined with Eric's to turn him into . . . this?" Manny said, pointing at the vine curled underneath him like a chair.

Frankie thought for a moment, tapping their foot on the floor. An electric spark shot out of Frankie's ear. "Me!" they shouted.

Clawdeen raised an eyebrow. "What do you mean, me?"

Frankie shook their head. "Well, not me exactly. But what kind of monster do we know that's part plant? More than that, what kind of monster do we know can change itself to look like a plant? Or maybe a tree trunk as it sits and waits for prey to hop into its mouth?"

"A sachamama!" Draculaura shouted, clapping her hands.

Manny closed the notebook in his lap. "So, Dr. Hemlock combined her own sachamama DNA with Eric's arachnid DNA in the hopes that it would increase Eric's silk production. But clearly it went wrong."

"The balance wasn't right," Twyla said quietly. "Too much sachamama DNA and not enough arachnid."

Thick vines in another corner of the room uncoiled, revealing vials and beakers covered in cobwebs.

"Just a suggestion, but maybe we could try remaking the mixture that Dr. Hemlock used," Manny said.

"I don't think any of us has a high enough grade in boo-ology to be able to do that," Clawdeen said. "Not even you, Draculaura."

Frankie dropped the notebook in their hands. "Botanist frontal lobe! Oh, and a cerebellum from a zombie mathematician. And a bit from a human chemist."

"I've been repeating myself over and over. Can no one hear me?" Twyla raised an eyebrow. "Only you can do this, Frankie."

Draculaura rushed over to the vials and beakers, brushing her hands over the cobwebs and cleaning them up.

"You're not gonna have to chop off a finger or drain your body of its blood, are you?" Clawdeen asked nervously. "Because I didn't pay enough attention during the impromptu surgery chapter of boo-ology. How are we gonna get Dr. Hemlock's DNA from you?"

Frankie patted the top of their head. "Well, my DNA is made up of all the parts that make me Frankie— a mermaid composer, a gargoyle seismologist, a chupacabra architect."

"And a sachamama botanist!" Draculaura exclaimed.

Frankie nodded. "Yep. My DNA will have part of Dr. Hemlock's DNA."

"But, like, no blood?" Clawdeen asked.

Draculaura rolled her eyes. "That's not the only place our DNA is."

"Spit!" Manny shouted and then immediately slapped his hand over his mouth.

Clawdeen looked at him, horrified, as he held out a vial to Frankie. "What?"

"You can get DNA from your spit," Frankie explained.

Frankie walked over to the large red flower on the wall. "Eric?" they said. "Do you mind if I take one of your leaves? Gotta combine it with my DNA. That might change you back into you."

A vine curled out at Frankie's feet and dropped a single small leaf.

"Thanks," Frankie said, picking it up and adding it to the vial that already had their spit.

"We should heat it up to combine it," Dracu-laura said.

Manny stepped out into the hallway and returned with one of the small torches that lined the passageway. He took the vial from Frankie and held it over the flame. The mixture began to bubble and liquify.

"I think it might be ready," Manny said, handing the vial to Frankie.

Frankie used a dropper to put a bit of the mixture on the vine. The leaves disappeared into the vine and the green shade changed to light gray. But after a few seconds, the leaves popped out again, and the color of the vine returned.

"It's not strong enough," Clawdeen said, groaning.

Twyla walked over to Frankie and put her hand

on her shoulder. "It needs to be supercharged. At the risk of repeating myself yet again, only Frankie can make this work."

Frankie held the vial in one hand and stared at it. They raised a single index finger, an electric spark shooting out from the tip.

"There's something I can do that Dr. Hemlock couldn't," they said. "Everybody stand back."

CHAPTER 18

ॐ 💀 ॐ

The mixture in the vial began to glow in Frankie's hand as small electric sparks sprung from their fingertips and danced around the glass.

Draculaura pulled Clawdeen and Twyla away as Manny took a large step back.

Bubbles popped up on the surface of the liquid as a bright blue charge swirled around Frankie's hand and over the vial. Frankie walked to the red flower on the wall, and the petals opened.

"Eric?" they said, holding out the vial. "This might do the trick."

A small vine curled from behind the flower and wrapped around the vial. Taking it from Frankie, the vine slithered toward the red flower as the petals opened like a mouth. Tilting the vial, the vine poured the electrified liquid into the center of the flower.

Frankie waited a moment, staring at the flower. The vine quivered and dropped the vial to the floor. The walls shook as the crawling plant slammed against stone, leaves fell to the floor, and a loud cry echoed from the flower.

"Look out!" Clawdeen shouted as a thick vine dropped from the ceiling and landed near Frankie.

The red petals shriveled from the flower and swirled in the air around the room. Twyla, Draculaura, and Clawdeen huddled next to each other. Manny hunched over them, forming a protective wall with his back and arms. Leaves, dirt, and petals flew through the room like a tornado. Frankie rushed over to the vines that were shriveling and piling on the floor, their hair whipping in their face.

"It's working!" Frankie shouted.

Vines from every corner of Monster High slithered down the passageway, through the walls, and back into the room. The pile of shriveled vines in the corner grew and grew as they pressed together and changed shape.

And then the wind blowing dirt and leaves in the air calmed. The room stilled as the vines stopped moving and fell on top of one another in a corner.

The only sound left was Frankie breathing as they approached the pile of vines.

"Help me," Frankie said, bending down and moving a vine aside.

Draculaura hopped up and heaved another vine aside with a grunt. Manny picked up three vines and moved them off the pile as Clawdeen moved four more. Twyla brushed several leaves aside with her hands.

And there, in the center of the pile, crouched on the ground with his hands covering his head, was a boy.

Eric.

"It's you!" Frankie exclaimed.

They grabbed Draculaura and Clawdeen's hands as Eric slowly stood up. He groaned and brushed leaves from his blue T-shirt.

Wincing as he raised his arms above his head, he whispered with a sigh, "Well, I guess that experiment didn't turn out quite as expected, did it?"

"You really got yourself into a pickle," Clawdeen said.

Frankie raised their eyebrow at her and whispered, "Clawdeen, there aren't any pickles here."

Eric looked at Frankie and chuckled. "Thank you for helping me. It's been . . . a while."

His voice was scratchy. Frankie reached out and pulled three leaves from his black hair.

"But you don't look any older," Twyla commented. "And it's been forty years."

Eric examined his hands and touched his face. He rubbed his forehead, the red mark of a black widow there once again. His spider fangs stuck out from his lips as he smiled.

"Is Valeria here? Did she finally figure out how to save me?" Eric asked, moving aside a shriveled vine with his foot and stepping toward Frankie. He looked around at the room, examining each monster standing around the shriveled leaves and vines.

Frankie swallowed hard. "She's not here. Part of her brain is, but she's not here," Frankie said, pointing to their temple.

Eric raised his eyebrow and looked at Frankie. "If you have part of her brain, does that mean she's . . ."

Frankie nodded.

Eric lowered his gaze and stood silent.

No one knew what to say.

Twyla walked over to Eric and stood next to him. "A friend helps you out no matter what."

A soft smile grew on Eric's face, and he nodded. "She never stopped trying to help me. Did you know that?"

"So she wasn't a bad monster?" Frankie blurted out.

Eric's gaze snapped up. "Why would you think that? There are no bad monsters, and, even if there were, Valeria wouldn't be one of them. She helped me even though it was making her sick."

Manny reached out his hand and helped Eric step over the pile of withered vines at his feet.

"Excuse me, but what do you mean it was making her sick?" he asked.

"Sachamamas need sunlight to survive. For photosynthesis," Eric explained. "All the time she spent in her lab away from the sun was making her weak. But she wouldn't stop. Even when her experiments didn't work, she never stopped trying to figure out how to change me back."

Draculaura cleared her throat. "Why didn't she tell anyone? Why didn't she try to get help?"

Eric shrugged. "That was my fault. I wouldn't let her. I knew she'd probably get kicked out of Monster High if anyone found out what had happened. I didn't want Headmaster Scorchson to do that to her. He kind of had a reputation for shooting fire bolts out of his eyes. It's always been just me on my own, so no one would've missed me. It was easier just to let the whole school think I'd disappeared."

"But they did miss you," Frankie said. "There's a whole page in the fearbook about you, and students wrote how much you meant to them all over it."

Eric's eyes grew wide, and a smile tugged at the corner of his mouth. "Really?"

Reaching down in the tangle of vines, Eric pulled out a notebook Frankie hadn't seen yet. He handed it to Frankie.

"She never stopped coming back to try to help me. Even after she graduated, she snuck back into Monster High whenever she came up with a new possible solution to my . . . predicament."

"The fact that she'd turned you into a plant," Clawdeen said.

"Yeah, that," Eric chuckled. "But then she stopped coming. The lack of sunlight must've finally been too much for her. I kind of just fell asleep. Until the school woke me up."

Frankie stopped flipping through the notebook Eric had given them. "Monster High woke you up?"

Eric shrugged. "It's like it knew something had happened to Valeria. And it didn't want me to be left down here forever."

Manny shook his head. "I think that's why the walls have been shaking so much. Your vines were pushing everywhere."

"And had anyone else seen doors pop up all over the place?" Clawdeen asked. "Like more than usual for Monster High?"

Everyone nodded.

"I wonder if we'd actually gone through those doors if they would've led us here," Draculaura said.

Frankie nodded absently, going back to flipping through the pages of the notebook Eric had given them. Their eyes grew wide as they scanned equations and experiment notes, diagrams, and charts.

"This is it," Frankie said. "This notebook proves the rumors about Dr. Hemlock weren't all true."

"What do you mean?" Clawdeen asked.

Frankie held up a page. "These notes show that Dr. Hemlock was trying to fix what happened to Eric. She was using different combinations of DNA that she thought would change him back. Even though Dr. Hemlock used her own DNA in her original experiment to increase Eric's silk production, it never occurred to her to do the same thing again as a possible cure for his predicament. These notebooks prove everything."

A loud scream filled the catacombs, and everyone jumped. Skullette's voice echoed in the chamber.

"ERIC ARACHNIDSON, PLEASE REPORT TO HEADMISTRESS BLOODGOOD'S OFFICE IMMEDIATELY BEFORE A HORDE OF WILD MOTHMEN HUNT YOU DOWN AND SNACK ON YOUR LIVER. OH WAIT . . . NOT THAT LAST PART. JUST GET THERE AS SOON AS POSSIBLE."

Clawdeen shook her head. "How does Headmistress Bloodgood even know you're here?"

Frankie put their hands on their hips and looked at the vines that had pulled themselves from every corner of the school.

"I think Monster High is a tattletale," they said.

CHAPTER 19

❦ 🐾 ❦

The group headed up to Headmistress Bloodgood's office. Several teachers were sweeping up bits of stone and rocks that had fallen when the vine that was Eric Arachnidson had crept through the school.

"Oh, this swirl of dust looks like a poltergeist I once dated," Mrs. O'Shriek commented as she pushed a broom across the floor in front of her classroom.

Coach Thunderbird chuckled, her whistle still dangling from her beak. "O'Shriek, I bet you sixteen zappaccinos I can sweep this hallway faster than you can."

Eric looked at the coffin-shaped lockers, the garbage goblins meandering around, and the groups of students hurrying to class.

"Not much has changed," he said, shaking his head. "Except for the new headmistress, the electric lights instead of torches, and those talking boxes all the students seem to be holding."

"The iCoffins?" Draculaura said.

Eric nodded and sighed. "So, yeah. Maybe a lot has changed."

When Frankie and Eric arrived at Headmistress Bloodgood's office along with Draculaura, Clawdeen, Manny, and Twyla, they filled the room. A few books from the headmistress's tall shelves still lay on the floor where they had fallen when the walls shook, and Mortimer the delivery dragon was working to put them back in their place.

Headmistress Bloodgood sat behind her desk and folded her hands in front of her. "This group has been a bit busy, I think," she said.

Draculaura bit her lip. "We were working on extra credit?"

Getting up from her desk, Headmistress Bloodgood shook her head and motioned for Eric and Frankie to sit down. "Nice try, Draculaura. Monster High hasn't been in such a state of chaos since Goobert's family decided to surprise him for his birthday and covered the entire school in green slime. So, tell me what you've been up to. *Now.*"

Frankie told the headmistress about having visions of Dr. Hemlock at school, and Eric confessed to the experiments he and Valeria had been doing while Manny explained searching through the catacombs and Clawdeen gave a play-by-play of fighting off the crawling vines.

All at the same time.

"Enough!" Headmistress Bloodgood shouted as Mortimer howled. "Frankie and Eric, you will speak, one at a time."

Manny slipped Frankie their research checklist, and Frankie cleared their throat. "It all started when you gave me the file that said I had a brain bit from Dr. Hemlock. I saw that she was a sachamama, but I wasn't sure if that was a good thing, since there are so many bad rumors going around about them."

Draculaura stepped forward and patted Frankie on the shoulder. "Remember, there are no bad monsters," she whispered.

Frankie smiled and continued. "I decided to research Dr. Hemlock as much as I could to see if the rumors about her doing experiments on humans were true. That's when I discovered that she was a student at Monster High and that Eric disappeared while she was here."

Headmistress Bloodgood nodded. "I do remember reading about you, Eric, when I took over for Headmaster Scorchson. Although his notes were half burnt and a little difficult to decipher."

Eric nodded. "What happened to me wasn't Valeria's fault. She was just trying to help, but things got out of hand."

Clawdeen chuckled and muttered under her breath, "Just a regular day at Monster High."

Frankie played with the zipper on their jacket, distractedly raising and lowering it. "She might not have meant to hurt Eric, but I'm afraid that the things she did to try to make everything better weren't right."

"What are you saying, Frankie?" Headmistress Bloodgood asked.

Frankie took a deep breath. "The rumors about Dr. Hemlock are true. The descriptions of experiments in her notebook show that she was actually doing experiments on humans."

Closing their eyes, Frankie thought for a moment. "I think she got away with it for so long because she had a Glawackus statue like the one at Monster High that makes humans forget they've seen the school."

"She did?" Twyla said. "I've read all about Glawackus statues, but I've never heard of anyone using them like that."

Frankie pulled out their iCoffin and opened up the *Gory Gazette* EekTok where the snake-looking man had spilled all the rumors about Dr. Hemlock. Over his shoulder was an ivy-covered statue that looked just like the one at Monster High's gates.

"That's how she erased the memories of the humans she experimented on, because she wanted to make sure they didn't remember the monster world. She was trying to keep us all safe," Frankie explained. "But I found some humans in the park outside of

Monster High who had part of her notebook. It was pretty graphic about the horrible experiments she was doing. It was all about her crouching over a human that was strapped to a table and extracting their DNA with a sharp needle. It was horrible."

Frankie sighed and shrugged their shoulders.

"That was a story," Twyla's voice squeaked from behind Manny.

"What do you mean?" Headmistress Bloodgood asked. She motioned Twyla forward.

Twyla's eyes darted to Mortimer and the fallen books before settling on Headmistress Bloodgood's hands, folded neatly on her desk.

"I've read a scene just like that before in a book of horror short stories. And the notebook I read in the catacombs didn't have any experiments in it at all. It was a horror story. But the handwriting was the same. Dr. Hemlock clearly wrote it."

Eric laughed. "I guess she kept writing those. She was so descriptive. Her stories were always easy to picture!"

"Dr. Hemlock wrote horror stories?" Frankie asked, their brain buzzing at the prospect of having not only a bit of sachamama botanist but also a bit of horror story author. Maybe their vision in the forest hadn't been a real memory at all, but one from the doctor's imagination.

Eric nodded. "Whenever Valeria got stressed out with schoolwork or just life at Monster High, she'd write stories. That was how we first became friends. We both wanted to read the only copy of *Tanglewood's Tales of Terror* and fought over it in the library."

Draculaura laughed. "Relatable."

Twyla shrugged. "I've read her stories before. They're in the library."

Manny's eyes grew wide, and he gasped. "V. H. Sachs! There's an anthology of her short stories in the fiction section. I think Twyla has checked it out twenty-three times."

Twyla rotated the bracelet on her wrist. "I like scary stories. And hers are all about an evil scientist."

Frankie checked their photographic memory and instantly saw the book Twyla had been reading in the library—*Thirteen Creepy Crawly Tales of Poison Plant Horror* by V. H. Sachs.

"Zaps! The humans!" Frankie exclaimed.

Draculaura raised an eyebrow at Frankie. "What are you talking about?"

Frankie smiled. "The humans I saw having a séance in the park, and then when we went to Dr. Hemlock's lab—"

"When you went where?!?" Headmistress Bloodgood yelped, her eyes wide.

Clawdeen chuckled and shrugged. "Oh yeah, that. Little field trip."

Headmistress Bloodgood groaned, her hand resting on her forehead. "Continue, Frankie. What was it about these humans you saw when you took an unsanctioned field trip away from the school and into the human world?"

Frankie closed their eyes and clenched their fists, replaying in their mind the séance in the park and the humans searching the lab.

"I've got it! The humans didn't have a page from Dr. Hemlock's notebook, they had a page from her short story collection. And they were searching her lab to find more of her stories, not learn about her experiments. They were trying to contact her because they wanted her to tell them more stories," Frankie explained.

"So they were just horror fans?" Clawdeen asked.

Frankie nodded. "To them she was a writer, not a scientist. I think it's pretty cool that she was both."

Headmistress Bloodgood pursed her lips as her ax-shaped earrings swung against her neck. "It sounds to me like Dr. Hemlock was surrounded by as many rumors as her sachamama monster form."

Before anyone could say anything else, Frankie's iCoffin buzzed in their hand.

"Oh no," they groaned, showing the screen to Draculaura.

"Another Toralei Eektok," Draculaura said. "She's been trying to spread rumors about Frankie by saying that having part of a sachamama's brain is bad."

Drumming her fingers on her desk, Headmistress Bloodgood narrowed her eyes at Frankie. "Ah, yes. Cleo has been showing me those. I never figured Toralei for such a riddle writer. Bullying has absolutely no place at Monster High, so I'm going to put a stop to Toralei's posts. Don't worry, Frankie."

Taking a deep breath, Frankie held out their phone and looked at Eric. "It's OK, Headmistress Bloodgood. I've got it. It's time to make an EekTok of my own."

CHAPTER 20

Mom and Dad, buckle up," Frankie said. "Have I got a story for you."

Frankie threw themself on their bed with a huge sigh. Watzie jumped up and licked Frankie's cheek as they settled in. Frankie's iBall sat on their desk connected to a call with their parents.

"Let's hear it, sweetie," Frankie's mom said, brushing her black hair over her shoulder.

"And I know you don't actually have a belt to buckle. That's just a phrase Clawdeen taught me," Frankie added.

Frankie's parents listened closely as Frankie told them what they learned about Dr. Hemlock, finding Eric, and turning him back into a spider monster instead of a plant.

"That sounds voltageous!" Frankie's dad exclaimed. "Our Frankie did all that."

"We're so proud of you!" Frankie's mom said, clapping her hands.

Frankie glanced at the door to the dorm room and saw that they'd left it open. They shrugged, realizing it didn't matter now if Toralei walked by and heard anything. Frankie had nothing to hide.

"You know, at first, I wasn't sure about having a part from Dr. Hemlock. I thought it might be a bad thing that a bit of my brain was from a scientist with a suspicious reputation—who was also a monster with an even worse reputation. But my friends helped me realize something," Frankie said.

"What's that, our brave bolt?" Frankie's mom asked.

Frankie shrugged and scratched Watzie behind the ear as he thumped his foot on the bedspread. "It doesn't matter where my parts come from. When you and Dad put them all together to make me, they became something entirely different."

Frankie's dad raised his eyebrow. "And what is that?"

"Me! Frankie Stein!" they said, smiling.

Frankie's parents looked at each other, and Frankie's dad nudged their mom with his shoulder. She grinned and wiped a tear away from the corner of her eye.

"We wanted you to have the best parts you could possibly have, because we knew you'd make them yours in your own special way," Frankie's mom said.

Frankie took a deep breath. "So, you don't regret putting Dr. Hemlock's part in my brain?"

Frankie's mom pursed her lips. "Well, I certainly would have liked to have learned everything about the doctor before jumping in and using a part of her brain, no matter how brilliant it was."

"We were just so excited. You know how we can get carried away," Frankie's dad added.

"I've never seen anything carry you," Frankie said seriously.

Frankie's dad shook his head. "I think in the future, we'll be more cautious with the parts that we use. We'll do as much research as we can. We're so sorry that you had to go through all of this because we didn't have all the information we should have."

Taking a deep breath, Frankie's shoulders shook slightly. "I think I needed to hear you say that."

"Say what?" Frankie's mom asked.

"Sorry."

Frankie's mom smiled. "We are sorry, our sweet sparkplug."

Frankie clenched their hands at their sides. "So is it OK that I was a little mad at you for giving me a brain part from a scientist with a bad reputation?"

Frankie's dad nodded. "Of course it is. Everything you've felt this entire time is valid. No matter which brain part it came from."

"It was all our Frankie, and it was all OK," Frankie's mom added.

Frankie smiled. "Clawdeen said I'm all my parts, one hundred percent of the time. I think that's pretty cool."

Frankie's mom smiled and clapped. "Absolutely."

"We read the *Gory Gazette* interview with Eric Arachnidson," Frankie's dad said, holding up a newspaper. "I'm so glad he got to reenroll at Monster High."

Frankie nodded. "Since he hadn't aged at all while he was in his plant form, Headmistress Bloodgood decided he could continue as a student here. Although no one is exactly sure how old he is."

The iCoffin in Frankie's pocket screamed, the alarm they had set going off.

"Oh, Mom and Dad. I gotta go!" Frankie said, hopping off their bed. "I've got a meeting with Draculaura's dad in the library."

Frankie's parents gasped and their eyes grew wide. "*The* Dracula?" Frankie's mom said. "You're making waves at school, for sure."

Frankie bit their lip. "I'm pretty sure Lagoona is the only one who makes waves. But I'll see you later at the talent show, right?"

"We wouldn't miss it!" Frankie's parents shouted in unison and waved goodbye.

Clicking off the call, Frankie skipped toward the library. The halls were finally clear of dirt and stone, something the garbage goblins weren't too happy about, since there wasn't any stray trash left to eat up off the floor.

Right before they got to the library, Clawdeen called down the hallway. "Frankie, wait! I've got one last clawsome piece of the puzzle figured out."

Frankie raised their eyebrow. "I didn't think we were doing a puzzle. I'm here to talk to Dracula."

Clawdeen waved her hand and smiled. "No, a final piece of the puzzle with Dr. Hemlock. I visited my dad again and went to that book club meeting. You know, the Bloody Brain Book Club."

"You did?" Frankie asked. "What did you find out?"

Clawdeen chuckled. "Well, not only do those humans *super* love horror stories, but they had no idea that Valeria was actually Dr. Hemlock. She was using the members of the book club in her experiments. She'd meet them at the book club and then coax them into her lab to get a small sample of their DNA. Then she'd erase their memory afterward, so they wouldn't know what happened. One of the members that we saw sneak into Dr. Hemlock's lab got part of his memory back, and he remembered Dr. Hemlock inviting him to her lab to see a rare horror book."

"So she wasn't hurting them?"

Clawdeen shook her head. "Not at all. I mean, it's probably unethical to take someone's DNA without their permission, but it's not like she was chopping them up into little bits and feeding them to a rabid sea serpent."

"Yeah, that's probably a good thing," Frankie nodded.

When Frankie and Clawdeen entered the library, Frankie saw Manny and Twyla sitting at the circulation desk reading a book together. Every so often, Manny would look up from the book and recite a few lines as if he was trying to memorize something.

"Over here," Draculaura called out to Frankie and Clawdeen, waving from a table in the far corner.

Frankie took a seat at the table across from Headmistress Bloodgood and Dracula, and Clawdeen sat next to Draculaura. Frankie tried to remind themself that the Premier First and Foremost Top Monster sitting in front of them was just their best friend's dad.

But the butterflies in Frankie's stomach still swirled around.

"Thank you for joining us today, Frankie," Head-mistress Bloodgood said.

Frankie nodded as their leg bounced up and down under the table.

Dracula sat with his back straight and his hands pressed on the table. His black hair had streaks of white on the sides, and his jacket was lined with gold piping. He was the fanciest monster Frankie had ever seen.

"Draculaura has filled me in on everything that has gone on here the past few days. Quite an adventure this school has had," Dracula said, winking at his daughter.

"But it was all under control," Headmistress Blood-good interrupted. "Always under control!"

Dracula waved a dismissive hand at Headmistress Bloodgood and looked at Frankie. "I think you are in a special position to help us, Frankie."

Frankie raised an eyebrow. "I am? I'm just sitting here. Not really in a special position at all."

Clawdeen nudged Frankie with her elbow and chuckled.

Dracula smiled. "You have part of a sachamama brain, a monster that we know very little about because they're so rare and secluded. I was hoping that you could tell us any information that you might have learned about sachamamas."

Frankie thought for a moment and then pulled their iCoffin out of their pocket. They opened up their EekTok account and slid the phone across the table to Dracula.

"This might answer a lot of the questions you have," Frankie said. "I made it with my new friend Eric."

Dracula tried to press play on the video but hit the wrong button, and a loud screeching sound filled the library.

"Dad, that's not how you do it," Draculaura said, taking the phone from her dad.

"Oh, you kids and your contraptions. In my day, we just sent a messenger bat," Dracula said as Draculaura chuckled and put her head on his shoulder. She pressed play on Frankie's EekTok.

"Hi, Monster High!" Frankie said in the video. They were sitting next to Eric in Headmistress Bloodgood's office. Draculaura and Clawdeen stood behind them, along with Manny and Twyla. "It's been a busy few days here at school, hasn't it? There's been a lot of rumors going around, so I thought I'd clear them up with my new friend."

Eric waved at the camera.

"Everybody has already seen all the videos Toralei has made about the possible sachamama at Monster High. Well, I'm here to answer those riddles for you. It's me!" Frankie continued.

Clawdeen raised her head and howled in the video, earning a hush from Headmistress Bloodgood from off camera.

"I have a brain part from Dr. Valeria Hemlock, a sachamama. And do you know what I've learned about sachamamas? They're patient, they have an amazing connection to plants—"

"And they care a lot about their friends," Eric added.

Frankie nodded. "They do! Eric was stuck in the catacombs of Monster High because of an experiment gone wrong, and Dr. Hemlock never stopped trying to save him."

Eric chuckled. "Sorry about all the shaking, everybody. That was my fault. But I'm really happy that Frankie was able to use all the amazing parts of their brain and finish what Valeria was trying to do."

Waving at the camera, Frankie smiled. "So, I'm proud to have a brain part from Dr. Valeria Hemlock, and I'm proud to have a little bit of sachamama!"

When the video ended, Dracula handed the iCoffin back to Frankie. "It really is special to have a monster as rare as a sachamama here at Monster High. I think my council will have to investigate this Dr. Valeria Hemlock more and see what else we can learn about her."

"You know, Dad, if you want to talk to a really knowledgeable monster researcher, I might know one," Draculaura said, nudging Clawdeen under the table with her knee.

Clawdeen stifled a laugh and muttered under her breath, "My dad meeting *the* Dracula? That'll be the day."

CHAPTER 21

❧ 💀 ❧

The day of the talent show had finally arrived. Every student at Monster High was talking about it. No one could concentrate in their classes, and all the teachers finally gave up trying to lecture. They released the students, and everyone spent the time fine-tuning and preparing their routines.

Frankie stood backstage. They peeked out from the side curtain and waved at their parents. The Doctors Stein sat in the front row, cameras out and ready to record Frankie's performance.

"Nervous?" Draculaura asked Clawdeen as they stood with Frankie.

Clawdeen shook her head and stretched her arms. "Now that the school isn't shaking nonstop, it'll be a lot easier to dribble a casketball."

"Yeah, and my voice sounds a lot better when I'm not trying to be heard over rumbling walls," Draculaura said.

The trio watched as Lagoona stood onstage, flinging her arms in every direction as streams of water shot from her palms. She danced around the sculpture that was slowly forming, and the whole audience leaned forward in anticipation. With a final swoosh of her hands sending the last details to the sculpture, the crowd gasped and clapped as Lagoona's crush was revealed to be . . . herself?

"I've decided that my favorite person right now is me!" Lagoona told the crowd. "I think I should be happiest with myself first before I go swimming after someone else."

As Heath took the stage after Lagoona, someone cleared their throat behind Frankie.

"Can I talk to you for a moment?" Toralei asked as Frankie turned to face her.

Clawdeen huffed. "No, you can't!"

Toralei rolled her eyes at Clawdeen. "I wasn't talking to you. I was talking to Frankie."

"I think you've done enough talking to Frankie and talking *about* Frankie," Draculaura said with her arms crossed.

Frankie shook their head. "It's OK."

Now that Frankie felt confident in each and every part that made them Frankie, they weren't afraid of whatever rumor or remark Toralei might throw at them. They walked with Toralei farther backstage.

Toralei turned on her heel and faced Frankie. "I owe you an apology."

"You do?" Frankie asked, raising an eyebrow.

Toralei waved her hand. "You know I do. I shouldn't have made those EekTok posts. I just got . . ."

Biting her lip, Toralei tapped her foot on the floor.

"What did you get?" Frankie asked.

Toralei sighed. "I just got jealous."

Frankie's eyes widened. "Of me? Really?"

Toralei nodded. "Look, I still think that keytar playing is something my grandmother would've done, but the way your parents reacted to it was nice. They really liked watching you play and cheering you on. I don't get that a lot."

Frankie shrugged their shoulders. "They'll cheer for you, too. You're going to do a gymnastics routine with Meowlody and Purrsephone, right? That sounds amazing."

Toralei smiled. "I think it'll go OK. We just don't have a special touch to our routine, you know? If only we had someone who could make it really stand out, our performance would be a lot better."

Frankie gasped. "There's someone I know who could actually help with that."

Toralei raised an eyebrow. "Really?"

Taking their iCoffin from their back pocket, Frankie sent a quick text. "He's a new student, but I know he's an amazing juggler. He could probably give your routine that eye-catching aspect it's missing. Not that anyone is going to be catching eyes. That might be a little too much for a talent show."

Toralei smiled. "Thanks, Frankie. I promise not to listen in when you leave your dorm room door open anymore. Unless you're playing your keytar, of course."

Toralei and Frankie turned back to the stage and watched as two students no one in Monster High expected to perform in the talent show stood behind a microphone.

Manny and Twyla.

His voice shaking, Manny rubbed the back of his neck and spoke into the microphone. "Well, hi there, everybody. I'm Manny and this here is my friend Twyla. Um, for our talent we decided to show you something both of us are pretty good at."

Manny looked expectantly at Twyla who was staring at her bracelet on her wrist as she twisted it between her fingers. Realizing the silence, Twyla looked up and loudly said, "Reading!"

There was a small trickle of laughter in the clawditorium.

Manny cleared his throat. "Right. Yes. So, uh, we both found a new author who we really like, and we thought we'd read you a short story that she wrote. Her name is V. H. Sachs. Not only was she a student at this school, but she was a brilliant scientist—and a pretty cool monster, too."

"A sachamama!" Twyla blurted out.

The crowd gasped. Deuce began a round of applause that thundered through the auditorium.

As Manny and Twyla read from *Thirteen Creepy Crawly Tales of Poison Plant Horror* by V. H. Sachs, Frankie thought about their own talent show performance. They tried to calm down the butterflies in their stomach, but a small zap shot from their finger and hit Toralei in the arm.

She giggled. Frankie had never heard Toralei giggle in their entire life. All several weeks of it.

"Frankie! You're up!" Clawdeen called. "They've finally put all the fires out after Heath got too excited about the story Manny and Twyla read."

Frankie gave a quick nod to Toralei and headed onstage. The butterflies in their stomach settled. Instead of being nervous, Frankie felt ready to perform.

Electrified, even.

After Headmistress Bloodgood introduced them, and Frankie's parents finally stopped clapping, Frankie squared their shoulders.

"I think I'm ready to show you all the things that make me . . . me!" Frankie said.

"Go, Frankie!" Deuce shouted from the back of the clawditorium.

Taking a deep breath, Frankie began to dance. They twirled two times and sent sparks out of their fingers when they raised their hands above their head. The audience gasped as bright fireworks lit up the air above them.

Wiggling their fingers, Frankie made the small decorative plant to the right of the stage bloom with orange and yellow flowers. "Thanks, Dr. Hemlock," Frankie said under their breath.

Clawdeen and Draculaura jumped out from behind the curtain, and Frankie leapt over to them. With a touch of their index finger, Frankie made Draculaura's shoes shoot sparks and lift her five inches off of the ground. Draculaura waved to the crowd as Frankie skipped over to Clawdeen, touched their finger to Clawdeen's waist, and shot a spark which spun Clawdeen around in a perfect pirouette.

Giggling and floating back down to the ground, Draculaura told the audience, "Most electrifying performance ever!"

Frankie continued dancing, swirling, and leaping across the stage. Twyla came out from backstage with a violin in her hands. She laid the instrument on the ground at Frankie's feet as they spun in a circle. With a wave of their hands, a spark shot out from Frankie's fingers and electrified the violin, causing it to play on its own. Manny passed Frankie their keytar and Frankie started to play a duet with the violin. Music filled the clawditorium, and the audience clapped along.

The rhythm of the song sped up, and Frankie spun on their bionic leg in a tight spiral. In one big finale, they shot sparks from their fingers that danced across the ceiling in a rainbow of colors.

The audience erupted in applause and shouts.

Draculaura and Clawdeen ran to center stage and took a huge bow with Frankie.

"Be yourself!" Clawdeen shouted, howling at the audience.

"Be unique!" Draculaura added with a huge smile.

Frankie squeezed their friends in a hug and waved at their parents. Clearing their voice, they shouted across the clawditorium.

"Be a monster!"

ACKNOWLEDGMENTS

I'm dishing out large scoops of eye scream to several people who helped bring this story into the world!

First, to my agent Stefanie Von Borstel Sanchez of Full Circle Literary, who always has my back. Thank you for supporting me and pushing me to try new things.

To my editor, the incredible Erum Khan at Abrams. Thank you for being my lifeline while I worked on this project. You deserve your own personal madre de aguas delivery monster for all the questions I asked you! Thank you for your understanding and care. You made this story a delight to create.

Thank you to Shea Fontana for creating a world where kids feel seen, understood, and encouraged. Thank you for helping me shape this story into what it should be.

Thank you to all the amazing non-monsters at Mattel, especially Elaine Gant and Stephanie Hammond. Your guidance on this project was invaluable.

As always, thank you to my writing crew—Natalia, Lori, and Amparo. Your enthusiasm and support always keep me going.

Of course, thank you to my two favorite monsters—my husband and my son. You're the reason I tell my stories. Thanks for always cheering me on.

Finally, thank you to all the young readers who've excitedly read my books and found a home in my stories. Let's keep having adventures together.

ABOUT THE AUTHOR

Adrianna Cuevas is the author of the Pura Belpré honor book *The Total Eclipse of Nestor Lopez*, *Cuba in My Pocket*, *The Ghosts of Rancho Espanto*, and *Mari and the Curse of El Cocodrilo*. She is a first-generation Cuban American originally from Miami, Florida. A former Spanish and ESOL teacher, Adrianna currently lives outside of Austin, Texas, with her husband and son. When not wrangling multiple pets including an axolotl, practicing fencing, and watching horror movies, she's writing her next middle grade novel.